He was completely naked.

"Shannon," he said with a growl. "I want you to leave this room right now."

"Or you'll do what?" It came out husky, a dare.

"I might not be responsible for what happens," he said darkly.

"We talking whips and chains? Or just some really intense one-on-one sex? Sorry, not up for the first, but I could *really* be talked into the second."

He whirled around, stared at her, his expression a classic of perplexed amazement. "There goes that mouth again."

She raised her head and looked right into his magical eyes. "What was that about my mouth?"

She watched the change in his gaze as it morphed from bleak and angry to something equally intense but quite a bit hotter. Then, as though he'd given up, he said, "This," and cupped the back of her head with one hand, used the other arm to pull her up to him so that her feet dangled off the ground, bringing his mouth to hers.

Dear Reader,

Years ago I met an extremely short woman with a huge personality. I disliked her on sight; the feeling was mutual. We were both members of a group, and when we discussed it later, we admitted our hatred was because we each wanted to be the star of the group and saw in each other a potential rival. That honesty, the willingness to admit our foibles to each other, was there from the start.

The dislike passed quickly, the group disbanded and we stayed in touch. She makes me laugh with her quirky humor and audacity, sometimes cringe at her eccentricities and often-brutal honesty. She marches to her own drum. I grew to love her. We saw each other through childbirth and miscarriage, love, divorce, illnesses and family deaths. She remains, to this day, my very dearest friend, closer than any sister could be.

When writers meet great characters in real life, the urge to portray them in a book is strong. I have wanted to do so with my friend for years and finally have with Shannon Coyle. She is a minor character in *One Hot Target* and *One Cool Lawman*. But this story is all about her, and my friend is pleased that, at last, she gets her own book.

Diane Pershing

ONE TOUGH AVENGER

Diane Pershing

Silhouette®

Romantic

SUSPENSE

SILHOUETTE BOOKS

ISBN-13: 978-0-373-27567-0
ISBN-10:   0-373-27567-6

ONE TOUGH AVENGER

Copyright © 2008 by Diane Pershing

Books by Diane Pershing

Silhouette Romantic Suspense

DIANE PERSHING

For years Diane made her living as an actress and singer. She was extremely contented in these professions, except for one problem—there was way too much downtime, and she worried that her brain was atrophying. She'd been a voracious reader since childhood, so she took up pen and paper and began writing, first for television, then as a movie critic, then as a novelist. She started her first romance book in the spirit of "What do I have to lose?" As an actress, she was already used to appearing foolish—what was one more time?

She was lucky enough to sell that first story and many more since. Along the way her books have won some awards, including a Golden Quill Award, an Aspen Gold and an Orange Rose, and she's been a finalist for the prestigious Romance Writers of America's RITA® Award.

Diane is happy to report that there is no more downtime in her life; indeed, with writing and acting—and teaching classes in both—she now faces the problem of not having enough time, which she says is a quality problem indeed. She lives in Silver Lake, California, with her two cats, Gilbert and Sullivan, and waits patiently for her human children, Morgan Rose and Ben, to give her grandbabies.

Diane loves to hear from her readers. Write to her at P.O. Box 67424, Los Angeles, CA 90067, or visit her online at www.dianepershing.com.

To Brenda, of course. I'm not going to get mushy; suffice it to say there's nothing like old friends—they're the best. And that's exactly what you are, my old friend and the best friend a person could have. Okay, just a little mushy. Live with it. I love you.

Chapter 1

Shannon Coyle was in a hurry. The truth was, Shannon Coyle was pretty much always in a hurry. She'd been born that way, according to family lore. Exited her mother's uterus early, walked early, talked early, skipped a grade in school, made it through college in three years and law school in two. It was just the way it was—some had an excess of energy, not to mention brains, and she was one of them.

Right now, Shannon was hurrying along Pacific Avenue, barely aware of the typical early morning dusting of coastal fog, on her way to open up the doors of the Last House on the Block, the small storefront she'd founded two years earlier. It offered legal and other services to the indigent and the powerless, and her position as its sole full-time lawyer carried a lot of responsibility with it.

And did she need to play catch-up this morning! She'd taken three days off—totally unlike her—for a family celebration up in Santa Barbara. Now here it was, six-thirty on Tuesday morning, and she was at least a day behind. She made a mental list as she hurried along: two petitions to file with the court, investigations to get under way, a new summer intern to supervise. Her heels produced a *click-click-click* noise along the sidewalk as she made a beeline for the doorway, her key poised to unlock the top bolt. But just short of the door, she stopped, her attention grabbed by what looked like a bundle of rags several storefronts farther along, partly on the pavement, partly on the curb. No, she realized as she hurried quickly toward it, not a bundle of rags. A person. Most likely a homeless person.

A *dead* homeless person?

Setting her bag and briefcase down next to the body, which was facedown, she reached over to place two fingers on the side of his neck. Good, she thought with relief, there was a pulse. A weak one, but at least he wasn't dead. When she pulled her hand away, she noted the blood on her palm. Now she saw what she had failed to observe right away—reddish-brown stains on the ground near his head. Matted hair covered his face, but she pulled several strands away and observed more bruising on his bearded face.

With a start, Shannon realized that—even in profile—she recognized him. It was the Man with the Haunted Eyes, as she'd come to think of him. The homeless guy she passed every morning on her beachfront jog as he sat on the same bench and watched the sun rise over the Pacific. He wore ragged clothing and both his hair and beard were black, streaked with silver. From the first time she'd seen him—a couple of weeks ago?—something about him had called to her. Two or three times, she'd stopped and tried to talk to him. Always, he'd answered in grunts. He never smiled, was always guarded.

But oh, his eyes! A pale silver-gray, nearly translucent. Beautiful eyes, really, and intelligence shone from them. But they were also filled with more pain than she could imagine feeling and still wanting to live. Shannon had tried to get him to talk about himself, but he'd pretty much shut the door on her efforts, so she'd stopped trying. Some of the homeless were beyond wanting their lives to be any different than they were, that she'd learned from experience, so it was useless to continue.

She hadn't seen the Man with the Haunted Eyes since Friday morning, and now here he was, beaten nearly to death. Probably by some gangbangers having a little "fun," or by a drunk whose secret rage grew with each shot of cheap whiskey, or even another street person fighting over turf—a shopping cart or small sleeping corner. Tamping down her own anger at the injustice of it all, she shook her head instead as she withdrew a sani-wipe from a package she kept in her purse and cleaned her hands with it. How she wished she could wave a wand and make all the violent and cruel, greedy and selfish people in the world go away…to an island or another planet. But as she couldn't do that, she could do the next best thing—be an advocate for their victims.

She pulled a cell phone out of her purse and dialed 911.

Where he was it was dark. So dark. Blackness swirled and whirled around him like a living being. Where was the sun? He wanted the sun, but it was denied to him. Which was only what he deserved.

Help me, Daddy.

Night then, pitch-black, no stars, no moon. And cold. God, but he was cold! Every part of him was shivering. He was alone and cold in the swirling night with nothing to cover him. No, wait… There it was, the sun. A strange sun, not round but longer, and barely visible behind a purple-gray mist. And not warm.

Help me, Daddy.

Had he traveled to outer space? Or his grave?

He heard someone groan. Was it him? It seemed to come from far away. The groan again. Yes, it was his throat that made the noise.

Help me, Daddy.

No, he begged the voice silently. Please, no more. Was there nowhere he could go to escape the voice?

Pain ripped through him. The sun—the light, whatever—got brighter. Bad pain, lots of it. That was good—it meant he was alive. Or was it good? Wouldn't he be better off not being alive, not feeling, not hearing the voice?

Help me, Daddy.

Another loud groan propelled him up through the gray mist, fighting up to consciousness. His eyelids felt swollen shut, but he managed to raise them enough to see a long rectangular fluorescent light fixture overhead. He was in a hallway of some sort. Shivering, he heard other voices murmuring, crying, more groans, not his. He closed his eyes again. Pain. It hurt to breathe. Shifting his head slightly—not too far; it also hurt to move—he forced his eyes open again.

There were others around, bodies in some sort of hallway. A hospital hallway? his fevered brain wondered…or the entrance to the afterlife? He tried to raise his head but searing pain made it fall back again. Better just stay still, he decided. He became aware of more pain, different kinds, not just in his head and neck. His back. His ribs. His wrist. It hurt to breathe.

Then…if he was breathing, he must be alive. More groans. From him, from others? He closed his eyes, returned to the dark.

Help me, Daddy.

Shannon made her way quickly down the hallway toward the emergency area, glancing at her watch as she did. Eleven-thirty. Her lunch meeting was in an hour, but she had to satisfy her curiosity about the Man with the Haunted Eyes. He'd seemed near death as the ambulance had taken off with him hours before, and she just had to see it through.

Of course, she didn't really know what she'd do if he was still alive, or even if he wasn't. Try to find out who he was? Search for a relative who might want to know what had happened to him? She would decide that afterward; for now, she was here, at the hospital where they handled emergencies in the Venice/Culver City area, and which was, conveniently, only a couple of blocks from the courthouse where she'd filed her petition this morning. It wasn't a big deal to stop by, see what was up.

Click-click-click. She was at the desk.

"Hi," she said to the person at reception, a sour-looking young man with acne and short, spiky hair the color of orange Jell-O.

His return gaze telegraphed total disinterest. "May I help you?"

"I'm inquiring about a man who was brought here about four hours ago. He seemed to be indigent and he'd been beaten pretty badly."

What else is new? his expression read. "Yes?"

"How is he? I'd like to know the status."

"His name?"

"I don't know."

"Are you a relative?"

"Just a friend."

The receptionist's bored expression shifted just slightly into mild disdain. "You're his friend and you don't know his name?"

Even though Shannon's irritation spiked, she told herself to be patient; she knew her request sounded weird. But she was never pleased when she encountered bureaucratic resistance of any sort, an odd little quirk in her personality.

She tried again, with a smile this time. "Look, I'm a concerned citizen. I was the one who found him. Just tell me how he is, that's all, and I'll go away."

"I'm sorry, we can't release that information unless you're a relative."

She stared at him a moment longer, drew in a breath, expelled it and nodded. "Okay, fine."

Whirling around, she marched over to the double doors under the Emergency-Authorized Personnel Only sign, punched her fist against the button on the wall that had the handicapped symbol on it and watched the doors swing open. The sound of the receptionist calling, "Hey, you can't go in there!" was soon drowned out by the *click-click-click* of her heels.

As she walked she was surprised and yet not surprised to find herself in a dimly lit hallway with gurneys lined up on both sides, all of them containing bodies in various states of ill health. Some groaned; some mumbled; one said weakly, "Nurse, nurse," while another croaked, "Help me." Dear God, it was a scene straight out of Dante's levels of hell.

Shannon always tried to be a realist; she knew emergency rooms were in short supply and that public hospitals were seriously understaffed and underfunded. And she saw by the official-looking people dashing by that everyone was doing the very best they could, but still...

Okay, this sucked, big time. If Shannon could have waved her magic wand there would be plenty of clean rooms and gifted doctors, with first-rate medical care for all. However, she had no magic wand—hadn't had one since early childhood and her one appearance on a stage as a fairy princess—so, firmly in the world of grown-ups, she narrowed her focus to her reason for being here.

She found the Man with the Haunted Eyes—eyes that were presently closed as he lay on his gurney. It didn't appear he'd been tended to yet. Dried and crusted blood covered his cheeks, his forehead, his filthy clothing. One eyelid was puffy and red; there were bruises forming on his neck; the skin behind the bruises was pale. Too pale. He was still dressed in his rags and had a thin sheet over him, but his body shook with tremors. She put a hand to his forehead. He was burning up. He needed to be seen and soon. Again, she stifled her anger. Everyone in this hallway of anguish needed to be seen, but she'd learned to pick her battles.

Click-click-click. At the end of the hall she found another desk with three nurses in flowered coats huddled around a coffeepot, all of them sipping cups of the brown brew.

"Excuse me?" she said.

They looked in her direction, then lowered their line of vision.

She sighed, inwardly, used to this. Yes, she was short, even in three-inch heels that hurt and that she wore only on court days, and which made her a whopping five foot two, give or take. She was short, she'd always been short, would always be short. It was her cross to bear because most people didn't take her seriously. At first.

The youngest of the three women said, "May I help you?"

"I hope so," Shannon said with a grim smile. "There's a man with major injuries and a high fever lying down the hall on a gurney. He's probably going to die if nothing is done for him and soon."

A taller, older nurse, the kind with a face that had frozen in disapproval somewhere around the Ice Age, took over. "There are many people lying on gurneys," she drawled in the voice of a heavy smoker, "and just so many doctors to tend to them. We're doing the best we can."

"Actually, the three of you are having coffee."

"It's our break. We get breaks and we need them."

"I sympathize, really I do," she said, meaning it. "I understand all about working real hard and needing breaks."

She snapped open her briefcase, found a business card and set it on the desk. "Please," she said, summoning up the closest she could get to a tone of calm nonconfrontation, "I would deeply appreciate it if one of you could take a look at this man just as soon as you're finished with your coffee. I'm his lawyer," she added.

She said nothing else, waited to see if the final sentence and its implicit threat of legal action did its job.

It did. The youngest of the three nurses, also tall but who had kind eyes and rosy cheeks, set down her coffee cup. She came out from behind the desk, looked down on Shannon from her much superior height, and said, "Which one is he?"

He raised eyelids that felt as heavy as lead, an act he'd managed to accomplish a couple of times before but had drifted back to sleep each time. Now, however, even though he still felt groggy—from fever? drugs?— he was determined to stay awake and take stock of his surroundings. His gaze shifted around enough to see that he was in a room on a bed partially closed off from the rest of the room by a curtain. From what he could tell there were other beds, other curtains. A ward, then, in a hospital. Light flooded the room from tall windows on the far wall. So it was daytime. Still? Or again?

An IV pole stood to his right and he followed the tubing to his arm and the needle inserted there. His left hand and wrist were tightly bandaged around a splint, leaving only the fingertips visible. He tried to raise his head but was aware of a brace around his neck. He ran his tongue over parched lips. He was thirsty. A glass of water with a straw in it sat on a table next to the bed, but he didn't have the energy to reach for it.

A movement out of the corner of his left eye had him slowly turning in that direction. A woman stood there, at the foot of his bed, watching him.

The woman was vaguely familiar, but he couldn't place her. His brain wasn't working too well—it felt heavy and slow. He tried to focus harder. Yes, he knew this woman, but it was her clothing that was throwing him. She wore a charcoal-gray pantsuit, a white blouse, pearl earrings. When he'd seen her before she was usually… What? Less dressed.

Frowning, he closed his eyes again, tried to capture a wisp of memory, but in the next moment it was gone. *Less dressed*. What a damned odd thing to think. Had he seen a picture of her somewhere in a bikini? In a magazine or something? No, not that. But what? And why was he having such a hard time concentrating? What had happened to him?

He opened his eyes again to connect with the woman's gaze. Her mouth turned upward slightly, she raised a hand and said, "Hi."

She was a little thing, maybe five feet. Not fashionably thin but not fat either. Short, curly dark brown hair, lively brown eyes. Early thirties, probably. *Cute*, that was the word. He had a sudden mental picture of a long-ago childhood friend with pigtails and freckles and braces— what was her name? Abby. Yes. Abby. Abby had hated to be called *cute*, would protest every time he'd said it.

But this wasn't Abby. This was…

He had absolutely no idea.

"Hey, there," the woman said, then followed up wryly with "I'm not going to ask how you feel because from the way you look, it's not too great. Do you know who I am?"

Not quite, he thought, but didn't say it out loud, just kept looking at her, wishing his brain would move more quickly, come up with some answers.

"Do you speak English?"

Again, he waited to see if his memory returned.

She wrinkled her nose, then shrugged. "Okay, then, I'll talk. My name is Shannon Coyle. I jog on the beach most mornings, and I've passed you quite a few times. You sit on a bench and watch the sun."

The sun. Light. Hope.

No, There was no such thing as hope.

Help me, Daddy.

Moaning, he closed his eyes against the voice.

"Hey, are you all right?"

Her voice was closer now, and he opened his eyes again. She stood near his knees, concern on her face. It was a nice face, pretty even.

"This morning," she said, "as I was opening my office, I saw you lying on the sidewalk. You'd been beaten severely. Do you remember any of this?"

Did he? He tried to concentrate, but nothing would come.

"Hablas español? Deutsch? Français?"

"Do you?" he found himself saying. It came out as a croak.

"Excuse me?" Her eyebrows raised in surprise.

"Do you speak all of those?" His tongue felt thick and he wasn't sure he'd made himself understood.

"Oh wow, you can talk," she said. A huge grin split her pretty face, and her chocolate-brown eyes danced merrily. "Amazing."

"Do you?" he persisted.

"*Español* only, and only enough to order margaritas and guacamole."

The way her face shone with humor made him think of sunshine. Now and when he saw her in the mornings. So he remembered that, at least. The jogger. Shannon Coyle in the mornings.

She glanced around, spotted a chair, walked quickly over to it and brought it back to his bedside. As she sat down, she said, "So, what can you tell me about yourself? Want to start by giving me your name?"

He thought about it. "No."

"You won't tell me your name, or you can't?"

His name. What was his name? Again, his brain couldn't come up with an answer. There were rooms in there, rooms with their doors firmly shut.

Through the haze in his head, he felt the first real hint of fear. Who the hell was he?

"Water." Again, he hadn't planned on speaking; it had just popped out.

"Of course. I'm sorry. I should have asked earlier."

She rose, hurried over to the other side of the bed, got the cup and held it to him, pointing the straw downward so he could sip from it.

The water was warm and definitely not from a high-priced, designer-brand bottle—and he didn't care. As he drained the cup, he was grateful to feel moisture returning to his mouth. When he was done, he pushed the straw from between his lips.

She held the cup up. "More?"

"Not now. Thanks."

She remained where she was, standing over him, gazing down on him, her bright, intclligent eyes filled with curiosity and compassion. There was a natural energy emanating from this small woman, even when she was still. It made him feel old and tired and depleted.

"Ready to tell me your name?" she said.

"My head is…filled with clouds."

"Ah. I see."

Shannon looked into the man's eyes. Despite the puffy skin and redness around one of them, they were still that strange, fascinating, silver-gray color and still filled with sorrow. She wondered if his answer meant his head was always filled with clouds, or just at present. Homeless people often went in and out of reality.

She watched as he lowered his lids, winced.

"Are you in pain?" she asked, touching his shoulder

gently and surprised he allowed it; from her encounters with them, most street people hated to be touched. "Do you want me to call the nurse?"

He moved his head side to side just slightly. Then he winced again, murmuring, "Go away."

She withdrew her hand. "Me?"

"No. The voice."

"What does the voice say?"

He didn't answer, obviously declining to share this with her.

As she assessed him, she was mentally ticking off the facts: Hears a "voice," head "filled with clouds," wears same dirty clothes every day. Most likely a paranoid/schizo off his meds. An all-too-common diagnosis among the city's homeless.

Shannon was aware of a small, sinking feeling in her chest. She was let down, disappointed to find out that the man in the bed was a classic example of one of the non-institutionalized mentally ill wandering the city streets of America. Deeply disappointed, in fact. There had been something about him that had been, well, different. The eyes, the intelligence that had shone from them—and still did. She hadn't wanted him to be just another statistic, just another victim of a social system gone haywire.

She cocked her head to one side and studied him, really *looked* at the man in the bed, which she hadn't actually done yet. They'd shaved him, probably in order to tend to his bruises, and now, able to see his entire face for the first time, it occurred to her that, objectively speaking, he was kind of nice-looking. No, more than nice-looking, in truth. In fact, he had the kind of face that, in ordinary social situations, like a party or in line at Starbucks, she would find, well, extremely *arresting*. A long, elegant nose, sharply defined cheekbones, a beautifully shaped mouth and firm chin.

She glanced down at his hands. Or, his hand—only the right one was completely visible as the other was bound up. What she expected to see were dry, flaked skin, cracked and bitten nails and deeply embedded dirt. But this man's hand, with its long, sturdy fingers, wasn't like that. There were no calluses and his nails weren't bitten or damaged. They were, perhaps, a bit long, as though they were usually filed down but he hadn't gotten to it lately.

What and who was he? Or what or who did he used to be, and just how long had he been on the streets? Was his break with reality fairly recent or long-standing? She wished she could see his teeth, so she'd know if he'd had good care somewhere along the way, but it was probably not one of her better ideas to push back his upper lip to inspect them, horse-style. Although she was sure tempted. One side of her mouth crooked up at the mental picture.

And then she stopped smiling. Okay, time to ask herself why she was putting so much effort into one of an army of the dispossessed.

It all came down to the same thing—those eyes of

his. They'd drawn her in from the start. *Why* were his eyes so sad, so haunted? There was a soul in there, and she was positive it was worth saving.

Oh, no, not again. Not one of Shannon's little rescues.

Her adored and adoring late father used to say that in mock horror. All of her family had made gentle fun of her for her "strays," but Dad had always led the teasing. Not animal strays; the people kind. She'd had a tendency to befriend kids who didn't have many friends—a severe stutterer, the socially outcast, those who were too skinny or too fat—and offer them her company and affection. Bringing them home for cookies and milk, playing with them when no one else would. Her *projects*, her psychologist mother used to call them, with a mixture of exasperation and love. The resuscitation of a human being.

But her family had never really understood her—she didn't pick people so she could fix them, or not only that. She was genuinely fascinated by outcasts. They thought differently, saw the world through a distinct set of glasses she didn't possess, and she was always eager to know more, about *everything*. And yes, they needed love, but then, she had an excess of it to give. It was a win-win situation all the way.

The nameless man raised his lids then, and he gazed up at her with those strange, pale, haunted eyes.

"Do you remember anything about what happened?" she asked him gently. "Do you know who beat you up?"

He mumbled something then, but she couldn't make it out. "What was that?"

She saw him drifting off again, so she leaned over and put her ear to his lips to catch what he was saying before he surrendered once again to sleep.

"Joe Don," Shannon said. "That's what it sounded like. I think."

"That right?"

"It was the weirdest thing, Mac. Joe Don. You know, one of those good ol' boy names?"

"Used to be an actor. Joe Don Baker."

"Before my time."

"Not mine," Mac said with a smile on his lined brown face.

It was later that afternoon and a shoeless Shannon was perched on the edge of Mac's desk, chomping on the baby carrots Mac's wife Wanda always sent along, in hopes that her husband would snack on them instead of the potato chips he was so fond of.

"I talked to the doctor," she told her investigator, "and the guy's injuries looked a lot worse than they were. Not life threatening, which is good. Concussion, sprained wrist, bruised ribs, lots of contusions, none of them deep enough to be concerned about. The fever will be gone after two days of antibiotics. And he says amnesia after a blow on the head is pretty common and he ought to be getting his memory back gradually, although he may never remember the exact incident."

Mac leaned back in his desk chair and stretched, the buttons over his stomach threatening to pop as he did. "Yeah. Had a few of those temporary-amnesia types back while I was on the job. Couple of 'em were faking it."

She took another carrot, crunched on it. "I thought of that, but, no, the guy was telling the truth."

"The cops say anything?"

"Don't get me started," she said with disdain. "Oh, sorry. Never put down the boys in blue in front of an ex-member of the species."

Mac smiled again, lifted a shoulder. "Hey I'm retired. I'm a civilian now. It's cool."

She swallowed the chewed-up carrot. "Well, I talked to the cop filing the report. As there's no name, no ID, no fingerprints in the system, he figured it was the usual—another homeless, wandering psycho, not worth the effort. He'll throw the report on a huge load of other files of unsolved beatings and that will be that."

"For the department maybe. But not for our fearless leader, right?" he said with a grin. Then as the front doorbell jangled, he turned toward the sound and nodded. "Hi, Callie."

Callie Kennedy, the Last House on the Block's summer intern, walked in and stopped at Mac's desk. She had to be old enough to be attending her second year of law school, that much Shannon knew, but she appeared to be about twelve. Skinny, nearly flat-chested, with long, straight, light brown hair and very pale skin, she rarely wore makeup and had a smile like an angel. That she intended to be a criminal attorney was interesting, and Shannon wondered if she had the spine for it. Callie had begun at the office the previous week, and her work was thorough and well thought out.

"Hey, Shannon, Mac," Callie said in her soft voice.

"Hey back," Shannon said. "Do you know where Lupe is?" she asked, referring to her receptionist.

"She had to go to the dentist. She left a note on your desk and the voice mail is picking up. Didn't you get it?"

"Haven't been to my office yet. Pull up a chair. I'm telling Mac here about this homeless guy I found beaten senseless on the street this morning."

"How awful." As she sat on Mac's visitor's chair, the young woman looked stricken, her soft hazel eyes large and concerned. "Is he okay?"

"He will be."

Shannon hopped off the edge of Mac's desk just as he said, "And I'm trying to tell her she did her good deed for the day, got him tended to, and to let it drop."

"And I'm telling Mac I can't do that." She shook her head, then cocked it to one side as she considered. "To be honest, I'm not sure why. There's something, I don't know, that doesn't add up about him. He doesn't...*reek*, the way some homeless people do. I don't think he's off the deep end, there's no smell of alcohol, no signs of drug use, his nails aren't damaged. None of the usual giveaways. He's a mystery."

"Joe Don," Mac said in his deep bass voice, searching in one of his desk drawers for something.

Callie looked confused. "Excuse me?"

"Could be his name." He drew out a small bag of potato chips and tore them open. "Shannon says he mumbled something that sounded like Joe Don."

Shannon snapped her fingers. "JonahDawn!"

Again Callie said, "Excuse me?"

"The cult. JonahDawn, yes! I've been after them for two years. It's perfect. I asked him who beat him up and I thought he said Joe Don but he said JonahDawn. I don't know why I didn't make the connection sooner!" Excited, she picked up her discarded heels and headed for her office.

Mac's voice stopped her. "Unless he didn't say that, and his actual name is Joe Don."

Turning, Shannon grinned. "I like my version better." She looked at Callie, enthusiasm building inside. "I'm going to need your help. Who is this homeless man? And what does he have to do with JonahDawn, which, my gut tells me, is one deeply evil group of greedy people masking as a religious cult?"

"What can I do?" Callie said, her eyes lively, a pleased smile on her sweet face.

"Let me do a little computer search and then I'll give you both assignments."

As Shannon took off for her small office and her computer, she was again stopped by Mac. "Can I play devil's advocate for a minute?"

She stopped in her tracks, turned around, one hand propped on her hip. "Go for it."

"You're going on one little mumbled phrase and trying to make it fit a crusade you're on."

"It's a worthy crusade."

"Come on, counselor, you have a hard-on about JonahDawn, so you're bending the facts to make them fit."

"May I point out that it's the homeless guy who mentioned the name, not me?"

"Maybe he did and maybe he didn't." He held up a placating hand. "Hey, Shannon, all I'm saying is you may want to step back and look for alternative theories. Is it that you want to help this guy or you want to get JonahDawn?"

As always, she was both irritated and grateful to have Mac's calm, mature voice of reason in her life, so Shannon considered his question. Then she nodded. "Okay. Got you. I'll keep an open mind, promise. But I have to tell you, it's in my gut that they're connected in some way."

"Oh, no," he said, with mock horror, his large brown hand over his heart, and sounding eerily similar to her dad. "Not your gut again."

"You wait, I'll show you!" she said with a grin, and again made for her office.

As she closed the door behind her, she heard Mac say to Callie, "The woman is the classic dog with a bone. She won't give up until she finds out what she needs to know."

"I want to be just like her. It's a wonderful quality," Callie said loyally.

"Yeah, well, depends," Mac replied wryly, "on what she finds out."

Chapter 2

"Hello?"

The sound of a woman's voice pierced through a dream he was having, and when he opened his eyes, the woman from yesterday—or was it the day before?—was there holding a camera in front of her face. She pressed a button, a small flash went off, then she lowered the camera and smiled.

He scowled. "What are you doing?"

"If we want to find out who you are, it always helps to have a photo."

"Oh. Yeah."

"I couldn't drop by yesterday. Sorry. Big emergency at the office."

"Oh," he said again. So, not yesterday. Two days ago. Or nights. Or whatever.

"You up for a visitor?" she said cheerfully.

What day had he been brought here? Tuesday? Yes, Tuesday. So that made today Thursday. Good work, he thought with disgust. At least his mostly vacant brain knew the days of the week.

"You look a lot better," the woman chirped.

Shannon, her name was. A small victory—one more thing he actually remembered. Shannon Coyle. Her suit was navy today, with a pink blouse, and there were gold hoops in her ears.

"They took away the neck brace and you're getting some color," she added.

"Am I?" Brilliant, he thought. Conversation worthy of NPR. Should he thank her for coming? Ask her why she was bothering?

"Look," she said, "I have a couple of questions, okay?" Without waiting for his answer, her head darted back and forth as she observed her surroundings, which included a loudly snoring man in an adjacent bed, his television tuned to a Spanish-speaking station that was even louder than his snoring.

She yanked aside the curtain of the sleeping man, picked up his remote and turned the sound way down. Then she returned to him—whatever the hell his name was—pulled up a chair again and sat down. All this she did with quick, efficient movements, as if she was in a hurry and needed to pack as much into each moment as she could.

She surprised him then by reaching over and using her fingertips to push some hair off his forehead. Her touch was amazingly gentle and he was horrified to realize that he nearly felt like crying, it felt so good. Ruthlessly, he shut down this totally unacceptable reaction. He *hated* feeling this needy, this weak, this defenseless.

"Don't," he said, jerking his head to the side but not before catching a brief glimpse of surprised hurt in Shannon's eyes.

"Sorry," she said, then returned to being the visitor-who-brings-cheer again. "So, do you remember what you said to me the last time I was here?"

"No."

"JonahDawn."

Help me, Daddy.

Pain speared through his head. He closed his eyes against the pain, against the voice. "Jonah what?" he found himself saying. The name sounded familiar, but it buzzed in his head like a fly afraid to land in one place.

"JonahDawn. It's a cult. You know, one of those 'We have the answers to all of life's problems right here' things. Spiritual healing, and so on."

He opened his eyes again. Something about her voice—she spoke as quickly as she moved, but it had a kind of musical quality to it—made his headache fade. "You sound skeptical."

"I am. Not of spiritual healing, per se." She grinned. "Hey, whatever works, you know." Then her expression turned serious again. "But of this bunch, yeah. Jonah-Dawn," she repeated. "The name ring any kind of bell?"

"I...think so, but I can't get hold of it."

"Don't push it," she said with another warm smile. "I talked to your doc and he says he's pretty sure your amnesia was caused by a blow to the head during the beating—and you had a heck of a concussion, by the way. But there seems to be no brain damage, which is terrific news. And your amnesia, well, it's not chronic, meaning it's not going to be with you forever."

"I know what chronic is," he snapped, surprising himself with how quickly he'd gone from pain to irritability.

She refused to be baited. "Well, good for you."

God, did she take cheerful pills? "I'm sorry," he muttered. "I know you're just trying to help."

"And I know you're grumpy and scared and not sure why this lady who tends to talk in run-on sentences is in your face. But, hey, you'll be okay, so that's good news, right?"

"I guess."

She cocked her head to one side, studied him a bit. "So, not to push, but do you remember anything at all?"

Not to push, said the most definitely pushy woman, he thought, and almost smiled. Shannon Coyle fairly hummed with eager curiosity, challenged by someone with no memory.

"You," he said. "I remember you, in the mornings."

Over the past two days he'd had several snatches of memory, quick scenes that went in and out of his mind, like clicking through TV stations. But the one vision that stayed and played out the longest was the jogging woman with the small, sturdy body and kind face who would pass him and offer up a smile as he sat on the beach. Once in a while, she stopped and talked to him. Said hello, asked how he was doing. The look on her face was caring, friendly, fearless. Compassionate.

She'd made the reasonable assumption that he was one of the army of homeless that drifted along the Venice, California, streets and made their beds in alleyways and under piers. She'd asked him more than once if she could help him, refer him to an agency, a shelter. He'd shook his head, never encouraged her to care about him, to take him up.

A do-gooder, he remembered thinking, a saver of humanity. The type who overflowed with love of the less fortunate. One who thought you could actually *do* something about the things that didn't work in the system. He knew the type—although he wasn't sure now why he did know the type. Had he had dealings with them in his past life? The life he still couldn't get a handle on?

He also remembered being somewhat attracted to her—how could you resist the sense of lightness and joy she emitted, so totally the opposite to his darkness and shadows? But more than that, he'd found himself reacting to her on a more primitive, man-to-woman level, which he'd viewed as an unwelcome intrusion, an assault on the carefully constructed wall he'd built around himself.

What he didn't remember was why he'd been on that beach, watching that horizon and waiting for the sun. How he'd gotten there. *Was* he a homeless person?

"You remember me in the mornings?" she repeated then nodded. "Good. I mean, not good you remember *me*, in any kind of ego-gratifying way," she said, laughing at herself. "Just, you know, good that you remember *something*. It's a start. Anything before that?"

He closed his eyes, tried to concentrate on some of the fleeting images in his brain, pictures without context. "A huge…house? Building? With turrets, like a fairy tale. It feels like a bad castle from a nursery rhyme. Or maybe I dreamed the whole thing." He winced. The headache was back. "No more."

A few silent moments went by before she asked softly, "Would you like me to leave?"

"No!" It burst from him with way too much spirit, shocking the hell out of him. "I mean…" He swallowed another strong surge of totally unexpected and inappropriate emotion. "I mean, I…haven't had any other visitors." And I'm lonely. I'm so damned lonely I want to die.

She sat back in her chair, crossed one leg over the other, nodded. "Then I'll stay."

"I don't want to keep you."

"You're not." She picked up a large canvas bag, rummaged around inside it and came up with a plastic bag of cookies. "My receptionist, Lupe, baked these. They're for you."

"How did you know?"

"What?"

"That I love cookies?" He took the bag with his good hand, and removed a cookie from it. "My wife used to tell me I was worse than the Cookie Monster."

Her posture stilled. "Your wife?"

"My wife," he repeated, equally surprised, rolling the thought around in his brain as if he were tasting a new flavor. "Blond hair, green eyes." That was it, one quick glimpse and then it was gone, like a snapshot deleted in a digital camera.

"Your wife?" she prompted again.

"I…guess I have a wife." He took a bite of the cookie but didn't actually taste it. "A wife," he repeated, trying to wrap his brain around it.

Shannon, who had thought her visit with the nameless man was going quite well, felt her spirits taking a huge dive at this news. A wife? She was hugely, disproportionately disappointed, she had to admit to herself. It was good news for him, of course, one more clue to his identity.

But, as far as she was concerned, it put him out of reach. Out of reach? Of what?

She caught herself up short. What had she been fantasizing about? *Dating* her homeless man? Becoming *romantically involved* with someone of unknown origin, most likely mentally ill, dressed in the same shabby clothing day after day, and who had been beaten bloody and left on the streets to die?

What was up with this? Where was her brain, her healthy sense of self-preservation? Had it been so long between relationships that she was shopping for the next one in a county hospital ward for the indigent?

Silly, silly, *foolish* woman, she chided herself, determined to get back on track.

She sat straighter in her chair. "So, you have a wife," she said with determined brightness. "That's good. Now we really need to find out who you are. The poor woman must be worried to death."

His brow furrowed. "I guess."

When he frowned, the crease between his brows was quite pronounced. He had Welsh eyebrows, she thought. Or Scottish. The kind that needed constant trimming back or the eye area reminded you of a terrier's. Not that her homeless man would remind anyone of a dog in the least. No. He was quite human.

And homeless or not, married or not, he was definitely looking better and better, the more they talked. More lively, less detached. More, well, yeah, attractive.

Darn.

The nameless man met her gaze, held out the bag of cookies. "These are really good. Would you like one?"

"I shouldn't. I brought them for you."

"But you will."

She grinned, took one of Lupe's delectable treats, bit into it. "Try and stop me."

One side of his mouth quirked up just a little bit. "You said you didn't bake them."

"I don't bake. I don't clean house. I pay others to do both."

This time both sides of his mouth actually curved upward, even if the smile didn't quite make it to the teeth-revealing stage. A victory of sorts.

"One of those, huh?" he asked wryly.

"One of what?"

"The non-domestic goddess type."

She gave an emphatic nod. "And proud of it."

She waited, enjoying their brief, mildly humorous exchange, eager to see if any other information would slip out, the way the wife news had. Instead, he seemed to go back into his head again, chewing slowly on his second cookie, his brow furrowed in thought.

Now that the neck brace was gone, she could see that, beneath his hospital gown, he was too thin, his collarbones too pronounced. He would need fattening up.

She tried again. "So if you remember me in the mornings, that means you also remember sitting and watching the sun, right?"

"Yes."

"Why? I don't mean why do you remember, just why did you do that every morning?"

He seemed to consider that for a moment, then said thoughtfully, "Life."

She cocked her head to one side. "Meaning?"

"To feel alive. I felt dead inside and the sun reminded me I was, in fact, not dead."

He had a nice, deep voice, she observed, very pleasant to listen to. "Why did you feel dead inside?"

This seemed to annoy him. "You ask too many questions," he grumbled.

"Just tell me to stop and I will. Although it won't be easy. I'm curious, big time, and I always have been. Mysteries fascinate me. Not to mention the fact that I'm a lawyer and asking questions is my stock-in-trade."

"Ah."

"You say 'ah' like you get exactly what that means. Are you a lawyer, do you think? Or maybe you just hate lawyers like most everyone else does?" Her question was good-natured and not in the least defensive.

Lawyers.

Something about that rang a bell, he realized, but it was elusive. "I'm not sure," he said slowly, "but I think I went to law school." He met Shannon's encouraging brown gaze. "Another of those brief flashes of memory," he tried to explain, "kind of like a Power-Point presentation, one illustration after the other, but they're mostly from long ago. Or I think they are. One of the images is me, sitting in a big lecture hall and it feels as though we're discussing the law. Or maybe I saw that scene in a movie. But I don't think so."

"Back east do you think? I detect a bit of New England in your accent."

"Maybe. It's possible."

"Do you have any recollection of why you ended up on the streets?"

"The streets?"

"When I met you on the beach, you had all the appearance of a homeless man. Ragged clothes, beard, long hair."

Help me, Daddy.

It came out of nowhere, the way it always did, and it made him recoil. "Damn. That voice."

"That same voice again?"

The headache was back with a vengeance. He closed his eyes against the pain.

But Shannon the question lady kept right on coming. "What does the voice say?"

She must think he was nuts, hearing voices. Hell, maybe she was right; the voice had been talking to him since he'd regained consciousness, and nothing he did could make it go away.

"You can trust me," he heard her say through the pain.

Trust her? Trust her with what?

Why was everything such a damned muddle? What had he gotten himself into?

He opened his eyes, gazed at her. She really did have the nicest face, and she cared, he could tell. Probably not about him specifically, but whatever he represented—one of the needy ones.

Ah, what the hell. He needed help and she was here. "It says, 'Help me, Daddy.'"

"Oh, no." She put a hand over her heart, obviously both surprised and moved. "How awful for you. Who is speaking? Do you know?"

"A child."

"Your child?"

My child, he thought.

He felt his eyes filling, his throat closing. Pain, gut-deep misery swept over him, invaded every part of him. He averted his head, blinked against the tears—he would *not* let her see them. He would *not*.

"Go away," he muttered. "Please. Go away."

"Me? Or the voice?"

"I can't anymore. I just can't."

He felt her small hand on his shoulder as it gave him a gentle squeeze. He fought the urge to reach up with his good hand and squeeze hers back. Flesh on flesh. The need to touch and be touched. God, he was so hungry for human contact. And deeply, profoundly embarrassed at how needy he felt, how exposed.

"I wish you could tell me your name," she murmured softly.

So do I, he said silently. Believe me, so do I.

The next morning, before the doors of the Last House on the Block opened at nine, Shannon sat behind the desk of her small office. Mac and Callie sat opposite her, both with yellow legal pads and pens resting on the desk. All three had take-out coffee cups in front of them, which Shannon had picked up on her way in as the office coffeemaker was on the fritz. There was also a plate of doughnuts, which Mac kept eyeing hungrily.

"Okay, gang," Shannon said. "Here's the thing with my homeless guy—actually, more and more I'm thinking he's not a homeless guy, not hard-core, anyway. Although I'm not sure why he was dressed like one, living like one. Hmm. Well, whatever, we need to find out who he is and what his connection is to JonahDawn. Mac, I need you to do a search for every time the name JonahDawn is mentioned in the past, say, year or so. Pull out Mrs. Greenberg's file—she was the one who first brought them to my attention, I think. Before you started here. She signed some kind of paper and they tried to foreclose on her house, and then when I got involved, they said it was all a mistake. And there was another case. What was it?"

"The runaway, the kid who left home and wound up there. Gertz."

"Right."

Mac nodded, made a note, sneaked a look at the doughnuts.

"Wanda said she'd skin me alive if I let you eat one of those," Shannon said. "Shall I hide them someplace?"

"Nope," the older man replied with a twist of his mouth. "I'll just hunt 'em down. Damn," he said with a self-pitying sigh, "but getting old is not fun, trust me. Weight gain, high blood pressure, high cholesterol. It's just not fair." He made a waving-away gesture. "Ignore me. Get back to the case."

Shannon nodded. "Okay, then, I'll bet the runaway and Mrs. Greenberg are just two of many victims. Let's get every article in newspapers, every interview, everything written about JonahDawn."

"Gotcha."

"Callie?" She looked at her intern and was, again, struck by how very, very young and very, very innocent she appeared. "Concentrate on my guy in the hospital. I visited him last night and, like I said, I got a really strong feeling that he's only recently homeless. There's no record of his fingerprints on file. I'm thinking that some—" she shrugged "—some trauma, illness, tragedy, whatever, brought him to the streets. He might have studied law at one time. He's educated, it's clear. Knows about PowerPoint presentations. There's a faint New England accent. I estimate his age as mid to late thirties. He has or had a wife, with blond hair and green eyes."

Even as she rattled off the facts, she couldn't ignore that same gut-level disappointment the news had brought her the night before. Which was ludicrous, to care about whether or not he was married. Just ludicrous.

"He might have or has had a child," she went on. "He hears a voice in his head, poor man, saying 'Help me, Daddy.'"

Callie looked stricken. "How awful for him."

Shannon nodded. "Big time. He wasn't specific about

the sex of the child's voice, he just stopped talking then. Oh, and there's a couple of pictures of him in my camera." She rooted around in her large tote bag, which was on the floor by her feet, and produced the camera, handing it over to Callie. "All of this is urgent. I'm thinking they won't keep him in the hospital too much longer and I'd hate to have him back out on the streets. I would do some of this myself but I have to spend the day in court in front of Judge McLaughlin, unfortunately."

"Your favorite jurist," Mac said with a grin.

"If you go for anti-female, anti-poor people, anti-anything but white and Christian, then yeah, my absolute favorite."

"You might get along better if you just smiled and said, 'Yes, your honor.'"

"I try, Mac, you know I do. But the man gets my temper up."

"No kidding," Mac said wryly, then rose. "Okay, I'm off to the library."

Callie looked up at him. "You can do all the searching you need on the computer."

"I know. But I need to stretch my legs."

"And buy something sinful at the bakery next door to the library?" Shannon said with one raised eyebrow.

"Who me?" Mac's deep bass chuckle accompanied him out of the office.

Callie stood, too, smiling now, practically rubbing her hands. "I'm off to my computer. I love doing searches."

"That's why we pay you the big bucks," Shannon said.

* * *

He was staring at nothing at all when two attendants, both pretty young but one short and skinny, the other taller and more burly, pulled back the curtain around his bed. The big one began to unhook his IV line while the skinny one tossed a pair of cotton pants, an old sweatshirt and a pair of rubber thongs at him. "Get dressed."

"What?" He turned to the larger man. "What are you doing?"

"Can you dress by yourself?" the first attendant said, as though he hadn't spoken, "or do you need help?"

"Are you taking me somewhere?"

"You're discharged."

"I am?" He sat up, pushed himself to the edge of the bed, dangled his legs there. Momentarily dizzy, he sat still for a minute to get his bearings.

"Gotta move it," said the skinny one, obviously in charge of communications.

He didn't like all these orders, or the attitude that accompanied them, but he had very little strength to do anything but what was requested. "Could you untie the back of the gown?"

After he did so, the attendant watched, his arms crossed, as his patient shrugged off the gown, then managed to get the sweatshirt on. It was enormous, but the soft cotton fabric felt strangely comforting. With his bandaged hand, it was a challenge pulling on the cotton pants, but he managed it, refusing to ask for any more help.

"Can you walk?"

"I think so."

"Good. 'Cause we're out of wheelchairs at the moment."

He slipped his feet into the thongs, stood slowly, swayed, got his bearings. "I'll be fine." His voice sounded weak to his ears. Hell, he was weak, all over.

"Let's do it." The talking attendant took off; the other waited around, watching him with disinterested eyes.

"Where am I going? Where are you taking me?" Hadn't he read somewhere about homeless people being discharged from hospitals and dumped on L.A.'s downtown skid row? Left there to die?

"A homeless shelter," the skinny one called over his shoulder.

"Oh." He was forced to put a hand on the big one's arm as he moved along slowly. He was out of breath, and the entire scene felt unreal.

Then he remembered Shannon. "I need to make a call."

"We don't got time. Come on." These were the first words out of the big one's mouth; his voice was higher pitched than expected, and he found himself having to stifle the urge to laugh.

As they led him away, he wondered if he'd ever see Shannon Coyle again.

As she pushed open the office door later that afternoon, Shannon was greeted immediately by Callie, waving several sheets of paper at her. "Got it!" the young woman said. "Your homeless man. I know his name, I know everything!"

"Seriously? Wow. Come, tell me all about it."

Shannon nodded at Lupe, their receptionist, and the elderly couple sitting on the reception-area couch, then headed into her office, Callie close on her heels.

She began as soon as the door was closed. "First thing I did was a missing-persons search, New England, in the past year, Caucasian men in their thirties—there were quite a lot of them, but I got a match—good thinking to take a picture. It's a pretty high-profile case, by the way. His name is Mitchell Connor, he's from New Hampshire and is some kind of big-shot business owner. His estranged wife and five-year-old son died in a drowning accident here, in California, down the coast near Carlsbad, about three months ago, and after that Connor went missing."

"Missing?" Shannon sat on the edge of her desk, took off her heels, rubbed her feet.

"No one's heard from him since. But it's him. Look."

Callie produced a copy of a newspaper photograph and Shannon took it and studied it. Yes, it was her homeless guy. Face a little fuller, hair quite a bit shorter and with an expensive cut. Dressed in a suit, with three other men in suits, all with small, confident smiles. She studied it some more. Even in the black-and-white newspaper picture, his eyes—pale and mesmerizing—showed up.

Wow, Shannon thought. Not only *not* a homeless

guy, a pretty successful member of the establishment. And, yeah, pretty darned good-looking, too.

All at once, something that Callie had just said registered. "The wife is dead?" she asked, thinking bad, bad, *bad* Shannon, to be relieved at the news. How low could you get, to be grateful that some poor woman had drowned? She was beyond help, a truly despicable human being.

"Yes. And the child, too."

Grief speared through her. "Dear Lord. That has to be the hardest tragedy to deal with—the death of a child."

"Yes."

"Is Connor a suspect in the deaths?"

"No. Apparently he was in Europe at the time, attending some sort of merger talks. He came out here, claimed the bodies, took them back east and buried them, and then just disappeared. Took a bunch of cash out of the bank and, pfft! Gone. Hasn't been heard from since, even though his board of directors sent detectives looking for him. The theory is that he committed suicide and his body hasn't been found yet."

"So he turns up here in California, a homeless man. Why?"

"Visiting the scene of their deaths? Lost his mind with grief?"

"Very possible. Hey, maybe the amnesia happened before he was beaten, a result of the tragedy. Wait, was the wife involved at all with JonahDawn?"

The outer doorbell jangled as Callie said, with obvious disappointment, "Nothing shows up that connects them. Or so far, anyway. I did a search with the wife's name and JonahDawn and came up with nothing."

"Both her married and maiden names?"

Her intern nodded. She was good, Shannon thought. Thorough.

"But Mrs. Connor and the child," Shannon asked, "they were here, in California, when they died, right?"

"Yes."

"Has to be a connection."

There was a knock on Shannon's office door, then it opened, and in came her tall, blond, flaky-but-street-smart sister, Carmen, carrying a large earthenware pot, out of which grew a small tree.

"Hi, Shan," she said cheerfully, then set the pot down in a corner, stood back, studied it, picked it up again and moved it to another corner. She studied this location, then nodded and turned to face the room's occupants, her bright, infectious smile beaming at them. Her outfit reflected her customary eccentric-yet-elegant taste—a long patterned skirt, sandals, a ruffled white blouse, open but tied at the waist, with what looked like a bathing-suit top underneath.

"See?" Carmen said. "I told you how great your office would look with a tree." At that point, she seemed to notice Callie for the first time. "Who are you?"

Shannon, who was used to her sister's whirlwind entrances and exits, could see from the expression on

Callie's face that she didn't quite know how to react. "Callie Kennedy, my summer intern, meet my extremely spontaneous sister, Carmen. She has a green thumb and does my plants."

"Hi," Callie said. "Pleased to meet you."

"Likewise." At that moment, Carmen seemed to notice that there were papers and reports on Shannon's desk, a file folder on Callie's lap. "Oh, did I interrupt anything?"

"Work," Shannon said dryly. "You know, silly, inconsequential legal matters, lawsuits, the usual."

"Well, then, I'll be on my way."

Skirts swishing back and forth as she walked, she went to the door, opened it, then paused and turned again. "Oh, by the way," she said with a twinkle in her eye, "you're going to be an aunt. Bye, Callie, nice to meet you." And with that, she was out the door.

"I'm what?" Shannon rose to her feet, bounded for the door and pulled it open to see Carmen's back exiting the storefront's main door. "When?" she called out.

"About six and a half months from now. Call me later," was the cheerful over-the-shoulder answer before her sister swept out in a flurry of skirts, the sound of the bell jangling in her wake.

Open-mouthed, all Shannon could do was stand, gazing after her. Carmen was pregnant. Ohmygod. Her baby sister was going to have a baby. Out of nowhere, a deep ache, a yearning that felt as though it had originated in her own womb, swept over her, making her momentarily light-headed. She held onto the doorknob for support, confused by her overly strong reaction.

She wasn't jealous, not in the least. She was happy, ecstatic, actually, for her sister and her husband, J.R. Couldn't wait to buy baby clothes and coo over the newborn.

But Shannon wanted that, too. A man to love, a baby to nurture. One day, she'd always told herself. Time enough later on, she'd thought. But now, hearing Carmen's news, she wondered if she was putting off something too important to ignore, and if so, what was she going to do about it?

Callie's voice interrupted her reverie.

"Shannon?"

"Yes?" She turned, looked at her intern.

"Shouldn't we be notifying someone that Mitchell Connor has been found?"

She rubbed a hand across her mouth, then her face. She was tired, needed to get a good night's sleep. "Probably. But, let's wait on that. I want to talk to him first. Maybe he doesn't want to be found."

"There's a reward for news about him. Fifty thousand dollars."

"Nice piece of change," Shannon observed, perching again on the edge of her desk. "The storefront could use it. And maybe we'll collect it. But not quite yet."

"Would Mac make some kind of comment like is that your gut talking again?" Callie asked with a mischievous smile.

"You got it," Shannon said cheerfully.

Lupe, a middle-aged woman with the broad features of her Native American/Hispanic ancestry, entered the office, holding out a copy of the local newspaper, a throwaway. "The ad is in here. It looks good."

Shannon took the paper and studied it. They'd placed a small notice about the Last House on the Block, encouraging those who couldn't afford to pay a lawyer to drop in. "Yeah, it does. Thanks, Lupe."

"Mr. and Mrs. Billman are out there. They're early."

"I'll see them in a minute." Absently, her gaze scanned the surrounding ads, then stopped. "Well, well, what do we have here? The JonahDawn folks. They're giving a talk tonight at a school auditorium. The seven moral principles of some name I can't pronounce. Looks like Bah-lin-du-lah."

"May I see that?" Callie asked.

Shannon handed her the paper, then glanced at her watch. She picked up the phone, punched in a number. "Hey Freddie? It's Shannon. Look, I have to work overtime on a case. Can we reschedule?"

Freddie's response was not pleased. Not that she blamed him. This was the second time she'd had to cancel him.

Eyes to ceiling, she said, "Yes. I know. Sorry you feel that way," and hung up.

"Did you actually have a date?" Lupe asked. "You made the time?"

"I should never have said I'd go out with the guy in

the first place. He whines. I can't stand whining. What time's the JonahDawn thing?"

"Seven-thirty," Callie said. "Can I come?"

"Sure. Lupe?"

"My babysitting night with my niece's kids."

Shannon hopped off the edge of her desk, went around and sat in her chair. "I guess you can send in the Billmans. Oh, and Callie?"

"Yes?"

"Wanna grab a bite and then stop by the hospital first? Meet my latest client?"

Eyes shining, her intern said, "I thought you'd never ask."

Chapter 3

He stared to his right, at the faded blue sheet that covered the window, not keeping light from coming in but affording privacy of a sort. Out in the hall, he could hear a couple of drunks arguing, rap playing in the distance. Through the thin walls he could smell onions cooking and old urine odors. At least he was in a room with a door, he thought, even if was only slightly larger than a closet. Anyone just out of the hospital got this room for a day and a night, he'd been told; after that, he had no idea.

Now he shifted his gaze to the cracked ceiling, trying to remember the dream he'd just had, the one that had woken him out of a deep sleep with his heart pounding and in a sweat.

No, not a dream, not really. A memory. A real one. Too real.

He closed his eyes, focused. He was at a cemetery. Two caskets, side by side, lay on the ground. One regular size, one tiny. Wind was blowing, leaves from nearby trees flying around, some of the female guests' skirts whipping around their legs. Someone else was trying to wrestle an umbrella closed. The sky was all gray. It was raining. Wet and windy and cold, it had been a perfect day for saying goodbye.

And for hating yourself.

Oh, yes. Hate. He remembered that day and how he'd felt—back then and today, too—his heart near to bursting with so much rage and shame and guilt, he thought he might die from it.

But no such luck. He was alive. But his son, his precious, sweet-natured, sturdy little boy, Jamie, was dead.

Help me, Daddy.

He had not helped his son…nor his wife, for whom he still had some feelings, even though the marriage had been dead for years. The marriage was dead, and so were his wife and child. Grief clogged every pore of his body.

"I'm sorry, Jamie," he murmured. "Oh, God, I'm so, so sorry."

"Hello?"

He came out of the swirling pain to look to his left. In the doorway stood Shannon Coyle. He was surprised and pleased to see her. Very pleased. Out of the chill into the warm. "You found me."

Walking into the room, she propped her fists on her hips. "And wasn't I pissed off when I found out the hospital had discharged you. They were supposed to contact me before moving you. On the other hand—" she waved her hand at his surroundings "—you're extremely lucky they found room for you at this particular shelter as it's one of the better ones. I say that with quotes around it. There's a huge shortage of aid for those who don't manage to pay taxes in our über-capitalistic city."

Her rant was obviously heartfelt; still he tamped down a smile at how very seriously she took her causes, and how very short she was as she spouted off.

A young woman entered, standing behind Shannon. Quite young—late teens, pale, no makeup. And way too thin. He stared at her.

Shannon yanked a thumb. "This is Callie Kennedy, my law intern."

"Seriously?"

Callie stepped out from behind her. "I'm twenty-three."

"Oh."

"And guess what?" Shannon said with a small smile of triumph. "We know who you are."

"Mitchell Connor," he said.

She looked taken aback then delighted. "So you remember?"

"Some of it. Since this morning. It's still in bits and

pieces but more of them now." A wave of raw pain hit his chest. "I remember that my wife and child are dead."

"Yes." Her brown eyes were soft, somber, filled with compassion. She perched on the edge of his bed, near his knees, patted one gently. "I'm so sorry."

"Yeah," he managed to say, needing to talk about something—anything—else. "If you found out my name, tell me what else you know about me. I can't quite put it all together yet."

She chewed her bottom lip before saying, "Maybe I ought to talk to your doctor, ask him if it's wise. It could be kind of traumatic to find out stuff you're not ready to hear."

"I'll take my chances. Tell me. I want to know. I need to know."

She nodded at her intern, who left the doorway, entered the small room and managed to close the door behind her. "You're the CEO of Connor-McCain Industries. You disappeared from New Hampshire three months ago, following the funeral."

"Three months ago? They died three months ago?"

"Yes."

"Where have I been since then?" he asked, horrified at this revelation, even as images flew into his brain, unbidden. Stately trees. A building, granite with large glass windows. A large room with a huge table in its center. Faces watching him, mostly men, a couple of women in severe business suits.

A white clapboard house with green shutters and a

porch. A little boy running up to him, a blue cotton Superman cape swirling around his narrow shoulders, arms outstretched. "Daddy, I need a hug." Picking up the little boy, twirling him around, the child giggling.

"My son is dead."

He wasn't aware he had spoken it out loud until Shannon said, "Yes."

She took his unbandaged hand in her much smaller one and gently squeezed it. At her touch, he found himself gripping her hand as if it were a lifeline. Which it was, when he thought about it. He had no memory of the past three months, was in a homeless shelter in a state on the other side of the country, and could have been just one more statistic. Instead a total stranger with a warm heart had taken him up, even though he didn't deserve it. But still he clung to this woman.

Somehow he knew he was not the kind of man who clung to anyone, not a person who professed need for anyone. But right now, he was all too grateful to have her, to have this small gesture of warmth, this human contact, because where his dreams and memories took him it was so very cold.

He gazed into Shannon's eyes, moist with tears for him. Beautiful eyes, caring eyes. And her skin, it looked so pink, so soft. He wanted to touch it, to run the backs of his fingers over her cheeks and down her neck, over her collarbones, to find out if her skin was as warm as she was, as soft as her sturdy heart.

"Talk to me," he said. It came out roughly, but he was

uncomfortable with the direction of his thoughts. "Ask me questions."

She offered a small smile. "You'll be sorry."

"Probably."

She withdrew her hand from his, put it in her lap. "Okay, what's the last thing you remember? I mean after the funeral?"

"You, in the mornings."

"That's it?"

"That's it. Then waking up in the hospital." Again he wondered out loud, "Where the hell have I been for three months?"

"It'll come. Any memory at all having to do with JonahDawn?"

"The name definitely rings a bell, but I'm not sure if it's because you've mentioned it before or if it's important."

Shannon watched his face carefully, looking for even a hint of recognition or emotion having to do with JonahDawn. "Nothing more, huh."

"Sorry. I know you want me to, but I can't."

"No. I don't want you to," she said quickly, filled with remorse. Was Mac right? Was she was guilty of trying to rearrange facts to fit a theory, something she was always accusing the police of doing? Callie hadn't found a connection between JonahDawn and the late Mrs. Connor, and Mitchell didn't remember. It was rare, but was it possible her gut had been wrong? She hated when that happened.

"So, listen, Mitchell—" she began.

"Mitch," he corrected, "to my friends."

Friends. She liked the sound of that. "So then, Mitch, we probably ought to call someone from your company, tell them you're alive."

"No." His response was quick and definite.

"Why?"

His brow furrowed. "I'm not sure. But I don't think I want to be found," he said, echoing her earlier notion. "Not yet."

"But you don't know why."

"No."

Callie, leaning against the closed door, spoke for the first time in a while. "But...I mean, shouldn't someone know? Maybe a girlfriend? Parents? People who might be worried, not knowing where you are and that you're okay?"

"I don't have parents. Not anymore." He nodded. "Yes. Not anymore. And no, no girlfriend."

"You're sure?" Shannon asked.

"Not completely. But if I've been missing for three months, it can wait another day or two, can't it?"

She rose from the bed. "Hey, it's your decision. First things first. We need to move you out of here."

"You're right," he said with an audible sigh that let her know how tired he was. "Hell, maybe I *should* call my company, tell them where I am. I guess I have money," he added ruefully. "I'll be glad to pay you for all the time you've put in with me."

"I didn't do it for money," she said quickly, stung.

"You still ought to be paid. You've been amazing. Thanks."

That was it? Thanks?

A small dart of hurt made her ask herself what was up. She'd been a good Samaritan; he was on the mend, had most of his memory back; he really didn't need her anymore, so why was she hurt?

"You want me to butt out now?"

"Excuse me?"

"You're talking about paying me and saying thank you, and you know who you are now, so I'm figuring you don't want me around anymore." She'd tried to say that last bit with off-the-cuff lightness, but she'd managed to let the hurt leak out, she could see it in his eyes, the way they widened with surprise. Oh, God, she could get lost in those eyes.

"It's not that I don't want you around anymore," he said. "No, no, quite the opposite, in fact." Much better, she thought. "But…you've given so much to me and I don't want to take up any more of your time." He shrugged. "I mean, why would you want to?"

"Because I do," she said, avoiding answering him. She glanced at her watch. She and Callie really needed to get to that lecture. "I wish I could move you now. Do you think you can tolerate a night in this dump?"

"Don't worry. I'll be fine. Go."

"Okay, then I'll be back bright and early tomorrow morning, and we'll move you to someplace safer."

"So, what? Are you my lawyer? I mean officially?"

"If you want me to be."

"Do you think I need a lawyer?"

"I have no idea. Either way, I'm not going anywhere. Goodbye, Mitch."

"Goodbye, Shannon."

Their eyes connected and something passed between them, something that made her hiss in a silent breath of wonder. Mitchell Connor and she were sharing a similar wave length. She couldn't wait to see what developed.

"Come on, Callie," she said, feeling thoroughly happy, "we have a lecture to get to."

Shannon and Callie had each taken their own cars and by the time they met up in the parking lot and then found their seats, the lecture had already begun. Actually, it was more of a concert combined with a good, old-fashioned revival meeting than anything else. The stage was bare except for hanging fabrics that burst with color, but professionals were in charge of the lights, which shifted and glowed and dimmed, taking on the mood of whatever was happening on the stage.

A group of white-clad, bald people of all races and ages was center stage, chanting, their eyes closed. The auditorium was mostly filled and half of the audience was chanting also. What they were saying was the name Shannon had read in the throwaway, *Bahlindulah*, which turned out to have the accent on the third syllable.

Shannon concentrated on taking it all in as the show went on. She'd met Jonah Denton before. Twice, actually, while representing her clients. Both meetings had been at his lawyer's office, and he'd been dressed in fairly casual attire. Tonight both Jonah and his wife Aurora wore long white robes with yellow and orange suns painted all over them. Aurora was quite a bit younger than Jonah, her ancestry somewhere in Asia. With her caramel-colored skin and high cheekbones, she was quite beautiful, like some kind of Indian high priestess. She was the only one on the stage with a full head of hair, long, black, exquisite.

Jonah's head was shaved but he had a full beard. Both had wonderful speaking voices. Very calm, no shouting, no yelling or exhorting. There were deep-breathing exercises, more chanting, a rousing song or two led by a couple of African-American women who must have been professional singers in their former lives. There were some children up on the stage, which made Shannon's stomach churn. There was nothing she hated more than seeing children being indoctrinated into anything before they had time to make up their minds.

The audience swayed, clapped, got into it. The message was that JonahDawn was the new beginning for all. The dawn motif, the chance to start over, the fresh day representing fresh possibilities for lives grown stagnant or dead-ended.

There were Seven Moral Principles of Bahlindulah,

who had been, according to Jonah, some minor god who should have been more major and now they were remedying the situation. From what Shannon could tell at first hearing, it was basically a hodgepodge. Some Scientology, some EST from the sixties, a little Baha'i, a little Buddhism, and just enough Judeo-Christian elements not to sound totally foreign to Americans. All of it was carefully crafted to appeal to those on the margins of life, those in despair or deep depression. Those looking for the Answer, those who believed that there actually existed the Answer.

Shannon, personally, did not believe there was any one answer to anything; all that counted was hard work and to be kind to others whenever possible. To help those who couldn't help themselves. To give back. And to have a pretty darn good time while doing all of the above. God might or might not exist, but Shannon was preternaturally allergic to gurus of any stripe, was the original non-sheep, non-lemming, never went anywhere everyone else was headed; it just wasn't in her nature.

Thoroughly detached, she observed the audience, darting glances all around the room, seeing that most people were hungry for answers, not to mention guidance. Looking for that perfect parent who would tell them the secrets of a life that didn't seem to make sense. Was *guru* she wondered, from the same source as *guidance?* Indian, Latin root? She would have to look that one up.

She glanced sideways at Callie, who seemed utterly enchanted by everything around her. She listened intently, closed her eyes and chanted when instructed to do so, and basically was certainly getting into the spirit. Uh-oh, Shannon thought. Maybe her intern wouldn't last out the summer after all. Darn.

Okay, then. If she hadn't gotten it before, she got it now. She was up against experts at exerting their influence on others. With money, a message and lots of gullible supporters. Well, she thought, mentally rolling up her sleeves, she could handle that. Shannon just loved a good fight.

Later, the only thing Callie said to her in the parking lot, before she got into her car, was "That was terrific! Thanks. See you in the morning."

Shannon watched her drive off, then, as she was putting her key in her car door, a voice behind her said, "Ms. Coyle?"

It startled her and she jumped. Then she slowly turned around. She was facing a very large young man, with a shaved head, a round face and small eyes. "Yes?"

As she said this, she glanced around nervously. There were not a lot of folks in the parking lot at this point, so she worked her individual keys in between her fingers, as she'd been taught in a long-ago self-defense class.

The young man's stare was slightly glassy, but didn't appear threatening. "Father Jonah would like to see you."

"Excuse me?"

"Father Jonah noticed you in the audience tonight and

requested a meeting with you. If you're willing, of course."

"Father Jonah?" What was with the "father" bit, she wondered. She hadn't heard him referred to by that appellation during the show. "Now?"

"Please. If you'll accompany me?"

"Where to?"

"He's backstage."

She debated with herself for a moment, but curiosity won. "Sure," she said easily. "What's your name?"

For a brief moment, he seemed surprised, then pleased, as though not a lot of people bothered to find out his name. "Louis. Louis Lee."

"Okay, Louis. Lead the way."

On the stage they were dismantling the hanging fabrics, packing them into long boxes. Shannon was shown to a small, plainly furnished anteroom off to the right. Jonah sat on a couch, his feet flat on the floor, hands on his knees, eyes closed, his lips moving as she came in. She wondered if he was actually praying or meditating, or if it was for effect.

"Father?" Louis said softly.

The great man's eyes opened and focused immediately on Shannon. With a warm, welcoming smile, he said, "You came."

"You asked."

"Thank you, Louis," Jonah said, dismissing him gently.

As the young man left, closing the door behind him,

Jonah indicated the armchair to the left of the couch. "Sit," he said amiably.

She sat, waited, wondering what this was all about.

"So what did you think?" he said.

"Impressive. How did you know I was out there?"

"We have cameras that roam the audience, to see if our message is getting through."

"Wow. That's quite a setup you have."

He offered up an apologetic, between-you-and-me smile. "It's a little on the show-biz side, I know, but that's what we need to draw them in. They've all been raised on music videos and MTV. They need the spectacle."

"I suppose so." Questions bubbled inside her, lots of them, but the one that made it out was "I notice that Louis called you Father Jonah. Do you have a background as a priest?"

"No. Some of the younger ones need a father figure—they either had none or theirs was abusive, so I try to fill in. Louis is the one who asked if he might call me Father, and some of the others adopted it." He shrugged, again bringing her in to his world. "It makes them happy and does no harm."

What popped into her head was the medical doctor's creed, "First, do no harm." How perverted that innocent phrase could get.

"So?" Jonah said, a look of expectation on his bearded face.

"So?"

"Are you, by any chance, thinking of joining us?"

Her eyes widened. Was he serious? Was this man on this planet at all? "I'm not sure what you mean."

"You were here tonight, listening intently, I could see you. I was—" he offered a modest shrug "—aware of a strong spirit in the audience, a new seeker." The light of the zealot entered his hazel eyes. "I was hoping it was you, Ms. Coyle, and that you were intrigued by what we have to teach."

She sat back, gave him an assessing look. "We've met before, right?"

"Twice."

"And each time it was, at the least, adversarial."

"At the least." Another warm chuckle was followed by a dismissive wave of his hand. "But we took care of all those matters, didn't we? Those misunderstandings? People not, shall we say, very sophisticated, who were confused by what we offered them? We made it right. No one suffered."

"That's one way to look at it, I suppose." She cocked her head to one side. "The other way would be that, by settling, you managed to escape harsher judgment."

"One could say that," he agreed easily, "and if my motives had been selfish or greedy, or even larcenous, I would have deserved that harsher judgment. But they were not."

He was good, Shannon thought. Really good. Attractive, welcoming, self-effacing…up to a point. Nary a hint of what she was sure was the evil in his black soul. She let out a sigh, shook her head.

"Anyhow, no, it was not me whose spirit you sensed. Although it might have been my new intern—she was totally swept up in the whole thing. She might just be your latest convert."

"Oh. Well, good. But I am disappointed. I was hoping… It's happened before. To me, for instance." A new light of enthusiasm shone from his eyes. "I was cynical and suicidal. A failure in every area of my life. I was certain there was no god, of any sort. How could there be, with my life such a mess? And then I met Aurora and it all changed."

"Oh? Is your wife the one who is responsible for—" she waved her hand around vaguely "—all of it? The seven whatevers?"

"No, no," he said, the first hint of a frown on his face. He was not pleased with her casual mangling of his creed. "The Seven Moral Principles of Bahlindulah were handed down to me, personally." The calm smile was back. "But Aurora was there, always, shining her light on my heart. Filling it with love."

The man was most definitely a piece of work, Shannon thought. Was it possible he actually believed his own bull?

She took a shot. "It was sad about Joan Connor and her little boy, wasn't it?"

Her gear-switching fishing expedition paid off, big time. In the space of a second she saw surprise, displeasure, then sorrow cross Jonah's face. He nodded sadly. "Such a sad event. The loss of two of our most recent souls. Our only comfort is that they are both now in heaven, spreading their light there."

Bingo! The connection! Yes, she thought. Her gut ruled!

She forced herself to keep her inner excitement out of her voice as she said, "It sure didn't hurt that Joan was a pretty wealthy woman, did it? Maybe a little extra cash in the JonahDawn coffers?"

The flicker of malevolence in his eyes might have been missed by anyone not on the lookout, but Shannon's antennae for phonies was set on maximum tonight and, oh yeah, she caught it. That hint of the black soul.

"I prefer not to think of monetary matters. I deal solely with our mission."

"Mission," she repeated, then offered her own version of a warm, just-between-us-grown-ups smile. "Call it whatever you like, Jonah. It's all a big con game, I know it and so do you."

She stood. Interview over. She met his now openly hostile gaze. "We're not done, you and I," she said before walking to the door then turning to add, "How about that homeless guy nearly beaten to death and deposited on the sidewalk near my storefront? Know anything about that?"

This time he was prepared. His face a blank mask, he shrugged. "We feed the homeless at our temple two mornings a week. Anything more than that, I don't know."

"Right." She reached for the door handle but was stopped by the sound of his voice.

"Ms. Coyle?"

She turned. "Yes?"

"May I offer a word of advice?"

"You may."

"Watch out for unexpected consequences of certain actions."

"How very vague of you. Care to be more specific?"

"With a lawyer?" A small smile flickered before he added, "I think not. Louis?"

The door opened so quickly, it was obvious the young man had been right outside. Eavesdropping?

"Please escort Ms. Coyle back to her car."

"I'll be fine alone."

"Perhaps. But I want to make sure you're safe."

She really didn't have much of a choice. The hulking young man stood there, patiently, and so she let him walk her through the dark parking lot to her car, her keys between her fingers again and prepared to run for her life.

"So tell me, Louis. Do you work for Jonah? I'm sorry, *Father* Jonah?"

"Work? Oh no. I am one of the Select."

"Excuse me?"

"The special ones, the ones who get to be nearest to Father. We're called the Select."

"How nice for you."

A small, shy grin, one that revealed a missing incisor

and a gold-capped front tooth, indicated that her sarcasm had gone over his head. "Yes. It is nice to be special."

There was silence for the rest of the short walk, until she used the key-chain alarm to unlock her car door and reached for the handle.

"Ms. Coyle?" Louis said from behind her, reminding her of moments ago when Jonah had done the same thing.

A small bolt of tension skittered up her neck. She turned, looked up at him. "Yes, Louis?"

"I would be careful from now on, if I was you." As he spoke an overhead light fixture was reflected in his small eyes, making them appear even more glassy and slightly deranged. Shannon swallowed down a sudden jolt of fear. Louis was the muscle of the outfit, she had no doubt, and he could crush her between his massive hands.

She stuck her chin out. "Are you the one who beat up the homeless man?"

His face went slack. He seemed flustered by her question, like an actor whose fellow player had deviated from the script. His massive body rocked back and forth for a few moments before he blurted out, "Is he all right?"

"Is who all right?"

His small eyes widened in horror. "No! I wasn't supposed to—"

And with that unfinished sentence, he turned and lumbered off into the night.

It was seven in the morning and Mitch was practicing walking with a much-used cane he'd been given, when the bundle of energy known as Shannon Coyle threw open the door to his room. She was dressed in an emerald-green sweatshirt and pants, tennis shoes, wore no makeup, and carried a shopping bag.

She came to an abrupt stop in front of him, set down the bag, folded her arms over her chest and gazed up at him, her eyes wide with surprise. And accusation.

"You're tall."

"You're short."

"I know I'm short, I just didn't know you were tall. You've been sitting or lying down every time I've seen you."

"Speaking of which..."

The energy completely drained out of him from circling his cot for the past five minutes, he lowered himself to the edge, blew out a breath. He was making progress, that much he knew, but it was too slow, damn it. He hated being weak, hated depending on others, even for the most minimal of functions. Hated it.

She plopped herself down next to him. "How tall are you, anyway?"

"Six-one."

"Oh," she said, obviously not pleased. Then she cocked her head to one side and gazed up at him, in that way she had of looking like a curious bird, and asked, "How's it going?"

He shrugged, feeling surly and irritated.

"You look awful."

"Thanks. I feel a lot better now."

"You know what I mean. Did you get any sleep last night?"

"It's pretty noisy here, so no, not much."

"More dreams?"

He nodded; dreams but no real memories. It was one of the reasons he was feeling sorry for himself this morning. All the blank spaces, the dark corners in his mind.

"Have you been eating? You need to gain weight."

The barrage of questions and opinions, well-meaning as they were, were beginning to annoy him. He ran his good hand through his hair, scratched his head. "Look, if you have your cell phone, you'd probably better call my office and let them know I'm alive, then we'll get some money wired and I'll check into a hotel."

"What would you do then?"

"Order a lot of room service, I guess. Get better."

"You know they're going to want to come out and see you. Or fly you home. There will be publicity. Reporters, probably. Paparazzi. Gossip, Internet rumors and blogging."

"Damn."

"You want all that? You want to go home?"

He considered this, then said, "No. Not yet. If ever," he added, surprised but knowing it was the truth.

"I'm thinking you're a tad depressed."

"Thank you, Doctor."

She grinned, undeterred by his sarcasm. "Hey, you can always count on me to state the obvious."

God, he loved her smile! It was like sunshine. He gazed at her, again curious to touch her, to run a thumb around her lips, which were slightly rosy and looked soft and welcoming this morning.

Before he could give in to the urge, and possibly make a fool of himself, Shannon, who seemed to have, even for her, an excess of energy today, got up, gazed around her, then back at him, with an expression of deep concentration on her face, looking through him not at him.

"What?" he asked.

She took another moment before answering. "Look, Mitch, I have an idea."

He waited, watched while her gaze shifted to somewhere in the vicinity of his chest. He waited some more.

Finally, she blurted, "Come home with me."

Chapter 4

"Excuse me?"

Now that it was out there, Shannon had no choice but to follow through. She met his frankly surprised gaze. "Have you regained any memory of where you've been these past three months?"

"No."

"Don't you want to know that before you resume your old life? I mean, what if it was something back there, in New Hampshire, that caused your amnesia? What if your life is in danger from someone back there?"

"Aren't you being a little melodramatic?"

She threw her hands up into the air. "You want melodrama? Try a major CEO gone missing after his wife and child died. Try that same CEO showing up dressed in rags a continent away sitting on a bench, then again on a sidewalk beaten nearly to death. With amnesia. Who doesn't want to go home again. I mean, come on—we could put it on the soaps today. Hey, Mitch, someone tried to kill you."

She could tell he really didn't want to think about this last part. "The police thought it was gangbangers."

"Because that's their excuse for everything. And to be fair, ninety percent of the time they're right." She shook her head. "But I don't think so. Not this time."

"No?"

"No."

"Why?"

She could have told him that, as of last night, she'd found the Connor/JonahDawn connection and it smelled to high heaven. But she kept it to herself; it was better, all around, if he remembered for himself.

So instead she told him what had been the truth up until last night. "My gut."

"Ah."

Shannon waited for him to pooh-pooh her answer; instead he surprised her by asking, "How good is it?"

"My gut? Pretty much right on."

"I see."

"Why aren't you making fun of me or rolling your eyes, like everyone else does?"

"Probably," he said thoughtfully, "because I trust my

gut, always have. It's why I became a success in business, so, no, I'm not laughing. And my gut is telling me to hold off letting the world know I'm alive and where I am. Just for another day or two." He closed his eyes, rubbed them with his fingertips. "The memories are starting to surface, I can feel them." He looked at her then and she saw all the exhaustion and confusion of the past week in his tired gaze. "I'm having these dreams, small glimpses that I can almost remember when I wake up. I think I'm close. God, I hope I am."

Now he scrubbed his hand over his cheeks, which sported several days' growth. If the full beard had made him look older, this look was downright sexy, Shannon thought. Although why she and most of the women in the world found a man in need of a shave a turn-on, she really didn't understand. Kind of a caveman thing? That element in the male of the species that refused to be civilized? Or was it the just-got-out-of-bed-and-why-don't-you-hop-back-into-it-with-me? thing.

"But why does all this mean I should come home with you?"

His question took her by surprise. "Hey, if you'd rather not—"

"No, no. I mean you're being way too generous with a stranger. I could be an ax murderer, I could be one of the most unscrupulous people in the world. A rapist."

She shook her head emphatically. "Uh-uh."

"How do you know?"

"My gut," she said at the same moment he said, "Your gut."

She grinned, and he actually let go with a little smile of his own, which made her relax a little. She plopped down next to him on the bed again.

"Besides," she told him, "I did an Internet search on you this morning and from all accounts you're pretty straight. You want the details?"

"Please."

"You're thirty-seven, no arrests, nothing more than a couple of speeding tickets. Graduated from Boston University with a degree in business, stayed on and did a year of law school. You left there, began to buy up abandoned factory sites that you turned into office space or malls. You formed a partnership ten years ago, bought him out three years ago. You're worth a lot of money, and at the time of your disappearance were in negotiations to sell it all to some huge overseas conglomerate. You always kept a low profile, not a huge social life, rep as a workaholic. Firm and fair but somewhat distant with employees. You and your wife separated over a year ago. And you're right, no living parents and you weren't dating anyone special when the—" she paused for a moment before going on "—when the accident happened to your wife and child."

"Accident," he murmured, his brow furrowed.

"That's what the police report said." She watched for his reaction because of course she had a few theories of her own.

"Accident," he repeated then shook his head slowly.

"That doesn't sit right with me. I wish I could—" He closed his eyes for a moment, then shook his head again. "Damn," he said with disgust. "It's so close."

"It'll come." She patted his hand.

He turned the full power of his gaze on her then and she had to catch her breath, sincerely hoping that she'd done so silently. Those eyes—clearer now, strange and silver, and still sad. Yes, and haunted. Had his whole life been one of pain or was this a recent thing? Could that melancholy quality in his gaze be simply a trick of his genetic inheritance, like some movie stars who appeared to be deeper and more world-weary than they actually were?

Either way, those mesmerizing eyes of his moved something deep inside her. Deep, *deep* inside. Out of nowhere, her brain flashed to Carmen's visit yesterday and her pregnancy news.

This made her jump to her feet, walk away from Mitch and stare, unseeing, out the small, sheet-covered window. Ohmygod, was her womb telling her that she'd met the father of her future children? And was that, on a purely animal, instinctual level, because she was now yearning for progeny and Mitch was the first man to interest her in a heck of a long time?

How long had it been since her last relationship? And who had it been with? She counted back. Bill Jergens, she supposed, which had lasted about a month or so. When? A year ago? More? Oops. Over two and a half years, since she'd quit her prestigious law-firm job, where she'd definitely been fast-tracked for partnership, and had instead founded the storefront.

Where had all her sexual drive gone? She was pretty healthy in that department, a normal, functioning woman. Sublimation, she supposed. Protecting and saving the downtrodden from the greedy bad guys took a lot of focus and energy and hours. Wow. Not until this moment had she truly realized that perhaps some of her family and friends might be just a little bit right about her—she needed to get a life.

"Shannon?"

Pasting a smile on her face, she turned. "Still here. Just got a little antsy sitting down."

"The thing is," he said thoughtfully, "I'd like to stay at your place, for a day or two anyhow. I just want to make sure I'm not inconveniencing you. I mean I'm not sure why you're devoting so much time to me. And don't give me the I-love-a-mystery answer."

A direct question, and one she'd been avoiding dwelling on too closely from the start. She sighed. Might as well go for total honesty. Well, *near* total, anyway. She clasped her hands under her chin and blurted out, "Your eyes. They're beautiful."

At his purely male reaction of horror, she moved away from the window and toward him. "No, I don't mean lovely beautiful. I mean they're...*astonishing*. Remarkable. And so sad. After we met, back on the beach, I began thinking of you as the Man with the Haunted Eyes. And—" She stopped, chewed on her lip.

"And?" he prompted.

She shrugged, thoroughly embarrassed now. "And I want to make it better, take the hurt away."

"Yet one more charity case for the do-gooder?"

She winced at his sarcasm. "Oh, God, is that how I come off?"

"Just a little."

"But you're a human being," she cried, knowing she sounded too passionate, too carried away, but unable to help herself. "You're in my life, you were dropped into my life, if you want to get all woo-woo about it, right onto the sidewalk in front of my office! That has to mean something!"

"Destiny?" The way he said the word left no doubt as to his cynicism at the concept.

"Could be. Or you could have been sent as a warning. I'm really not sure. All I know is that I need to see this through. See *you* through."

"To what?"

"To helping you heal. You can barely walk, you need lots of rest. And we need to find out why you're here, in California, recovering from a beating, and unwilling to let people who must be worried sick about you know it. And you'll be safe at my place. Anonymous."

He studied her some more, as though searching for signs of her complete sincerity. Then he expelled a weary sigh. "All right. I gladly accept your kind invitation. But you may regret it. From what I remember I'm not a good patient and I hate being fussed over."

"Then you'll get better quicker so you don't have to put up with that. Oh, goody, do I get to bathe you?"

The minute she said it she put her hand over her mouth in horror, knowing she was actually blushing. "I didn't just say that, did I?"

"Yeah, you did."

Now, that iridescent silver gaze of his was not sad in the least; instead she saw amusement, appreciation and, yes, most definitely awareness. Of her. As a woman. Which threw her for a moment because she'd been having this kind of fantasy crush on her homeless guy and now here it was and he wasn't homeless and it was no longer a fantasy.

And this morning, in a homeless shelter of all places, a whole new world filled with all new possibilities had just opened up.

"Okay, enough with the cute banter," she said, waving a hand in front of her heated face. "I'm embarrassing myself." She picked up the shopping bag and tossed it on the bed. "There's some clean sweats in there. Let's get you out of here."

She lived in a high-rise in Marina del Rey; a light-filled, two-bedroom condo that overlooked a harbor where every kind of craft, from simple fishing boats to extremely large yachts, were docked. God, Mitch thought, breathing in the clean, fresh ocean air, but it felt good to be away from the hospital and the shelter! Even if, as Shannon showed him around the place, he needed to use his cane for support. He was impatient for the day he could throw the damn thing away.

Her furniture, he noticed, was like her clothing— of good quality but lacking in any kind of personal flair. She had all the flair necessary, he imagined, unable to think about the scene back at the shelter and her bath comment without smiling. Shannon Coyle was some kind of miracle worker. He'd been dead inside, that much he remembered from his mornings watching the sun. Had wanted to *be* dead but lacked the will to carry it through. And then he'd met this energetic, nosy, opinionated, compassionate legal eagle, and now he didn't feel quite so dead inside, and it was because she was in his life. Maybe some of that joyful vitality she radiated had made its way into his own bloodstream.

There was only one bathroom in the condo, for which she apologized, quickly pulling down a couple of bras and panties from the shower rod. The room emitted that particular female smell, a mixture of bath oils and makeup, soaps and deodorant. It filled his senses and he welcomed it. This past week, all the odors he'd encountered had been medicinal or the reek of unwashed bodies.

It interested him that for a straight-ahead, suit-or-sweats-wearing kind of woman, she sure did favor sexy underwear. One pink set, one cream set. Low-cut bras and high-cut panties. Sheer and silky. He felt himself responding physically, which pleased him on one hand, but also made him wonder what he'd gotten himself into by staying with her and courting temptation. He had nothing to give a woman, nothing at all.

He followed her into the kitchen, where he lowered himself onto a ladder-back chair and watched as she opened up the refrigerator and leaned over to check out what was inside. Which drew his attention to her buttocks. They were firm—all that running, he supposed—but it wasn't a tiny rear end. No, it was generous, the kind a man could really get a grip on while pouring himself into a woman.

"I didn't prepare," she was saying. "I'm so sorry. I'll bring in some food for tonight. In the meantime there's muffins, or actually muffin tops, juice, an apple. Some leftover Chinese." She took out a carton, opened it, sniffed. "Nope," she said and tossed it into a tall garbage can. She took out another couple of boxes and containers, sniffed those, said, "Nope," again, then turned to face him with an apologetic smile. "I don't think I ever realized how sad the state of my refrigerator is. Sorry."

"No problem," he said, schooling his face not to show the lascivious direction of his most recent thoughts and hoping his seated position accomplished the same for the rest of him. "I'm not very hungry."

"But we need to put some weight on you."

"You really are a mother hen, aren't you?"

Her smile was rueful. "Guilty as charged. And it's okay, tell me when to stop clucking—I have no boundaries that way."

"Taking care of the whole world. Your shoulders must get tired carrying all that weight."

"That's why I run in the mornings, to shake off the world and all its cares."

"We are so opposite," he said thoughtfully. "I've been so hell-bent on success, I've never given much thought to the rest of the world, and you care enough for both of us."

Head cocked to one side, she said, "I suspect the secret to a good life is somewhere in between."

"But we don't do 'in between' very well, do we, either of us."

"No. We don't."

They exchanged a smile for a nice, quiet moment before Shannon clapped her hands. "Okay, enough chatter. We need to get you into bed."

"Why don't we do just that," he said, amused all over again.

As she watched while Mitch—disdaining her help— got himself into bed, Shannon pondered the several uses of the word *we* and found it downright thrilling. *Was* this the beginning of something? Something that involved the first-person plural? Something mutual, which, at the least, had the potential for sex between consenting adults, and at the most… Well, who knew?

In one way, Mitch fit a lifelong pattern of hers— she'd always been a sucker for men with great inner sorrow. But her romantic history told the same tale time and again: when the man in her life began to cling too much, she began to feel more maternal than sexual, a definite damper on the fires of passion. Eventually, she released them gently and sent them on their way, heaving a sigh of relief and pleased to be unattached again.

So her attraction to Mitch made sense. He was vulnerable; he needed her.

But it didn't make sense because he didn't want to need her and would stop needing her as soon as he was better. And he would never be the type to cling. Quite the opposite, in fact.

Hmm. This bore more thinking about, most definitely.

But not at this moment. She bustled back to the kitchen, put together a tray consisting of three pumpkin muffin tops, butter, juice, an unopened package of Swiss cheese and three cookies. She hurried into his room, where he lay beneath the covers, and set the tray down on the table next to his bed. He looked drained—the move from the shelter had been hard on him. "Look, I have to get ready to go to the office."

"You don't take Saturdays off?"

"Sometimes yes, sometimes no. But my office staff and I are having a meeting in—" she looked at her watch "—oops! Twenty minutes. Eat, okay?"

She dashed into her room, threw on some slacks and a lightweight sweater and hurried back to Mitch, half expecting him to be snoring away. Instead, he had the tray on his lap and was chewing, not with great enthusiasm, but at least he was doing it.

"Hey," she said. "I actually have some yummy stuff in the freezer. Lasagna, great soup. My mom loads me up every time I go see her in Santa Barbara and I was just there. You can defrost in a microwave?"

"I can probably manage," he said dryly.

"You're okay to get around with your cane?"

"Definitely. Go."

"I'll be back in the late afternoon. I put a card with all my numbers on the table."

"Got it."

She needed to get out of there, really she did. Instead, moved by a sudden surge of tenderness, she leaned over and pushed some wayward locks of hair off his forehead. "You need a haircut," she said.

He could also use a shave and would probably welcome a bath. This reminded her of what she'd said back at the shelter, which made her squirm inside all over again. She removed her hand but he caught it and held on to it.

"Shannon?"

"Yes?"

"Thank you."

She shrugged. "Hey, no big deal."

"Yeah, it is."

With a small smile, he pulled her toward him again and kissed her. His mouth was both firm and soft, and she barely had time to register pleasure at the quick flick of his tongue around her lips before he broke the kiss. "Go."

Her fingertips flew to her mouth, which tingled from his touch. "What was that for?"

"An impulse."

"Oh." Flustered, she glanced again at her watch. "Um, I have to go." She turned to leave but was stopped by the sound of his voice.

"One more thing."

"Hmm?"

"Why muffin tops only?"

"They're the best part. Why even bother with the rest?"

She grinned and scurried out the door.

Mitch watched her go, still feeling that sense of lightness she inspired in him, and not at all sorry he'd kissed her—hell, he'd been fantasizing about it for a while. She had a very kissable mouth, as he'd suspected, and an extremely kissable body. The sweater and slacks she'd been wearing let him see, for the first time, the small, round, high breasts, a narrow waistline and flaring hips. A small, compact, but hourglass-shaped body. A turn-on, for sure. He wondered how it might feel to plunge himself into all that energy of hers and felt his own body harden at the thought.

Reality clamped down on him. He really couldn't go there, he told himself, couldn't give in to his sexual impulses when it came to Shannon Coyle. It wasn't fair to her. She was so accessible, so open. So trusting. Too trusting. What was it that made Shannon Coyle tick? Internet search on his background or not, she still should not have allowed a total stranger in her house.

On the other hand, what kind of threat did he pose? Not much of a one, for sure. He was no use to anyone now, was he? She had to serve him, feed him, even clothe him.

His mood shifted abruptly to thorough self-disgust. Mitch didn't react well to being helpless. A loner and lifelong self-starter, he did for himself and didn't delegate well. When his business had begun to grow so fast, he'd had a lot of trouble with that personality trait. Handing over responsibility to others, trusting them to get it done right. Trouble with trusting anyone, ever, period.

Trust. That look in Jamie's eyes as he held his small arms up and demanded, "Hug." So trusting, so adoring of his daddy. All things shiny and wonderful in his daddy.

The sudden surge of grief that flooded him almost did him in. He managed to ease the tray off his lap and leaned back against the pillows. The pain of loss and despair sat in his chest so heavily that it nearly crushed him. He closed his eyes. His baby, his little boy, his little Jamie. *Oh God, the pain.* He needed release from the pain or he just might die from it.

Tears gathered behind his lids and for once he didn't fight them. He never cried. It wasn't manly, that had been pounded into him from childhood. Could he finally let it out? Would he let himself?

Why, in a condo in Southern California that belonged to a busy, short, way too intense woman he'd met only days ago, was he feeling that he was finally in a place where he could let go, where he could do what he'd never done in his life before, not even as a child—weep uncontrollably?

But it didn't matter why, and soon he stopped asking and just did.

Shannon scurried into the office a few minutes late to find Mac and Callie—and even Lupe—already there, sitting around the coffee table and two love seats that served as the reception area, drinking fresh coffee from a new coffeepot, a plate of bagels and cream cheese on the table.

"Sorry," Shannon said, "I got held up."

She didn't tell them why or who her new houseguest was because both Lupe and Mac would be concerned and she didn't feel like a well-meaning lecture this morning.

Not after that sudden and totally unexpected kiss, which had notched up the whatever-it-was between her and Mitch Connor.

"Hey, you're allowed," Mac said easily, spreading a thick layer of cream cheese on one half of a bagel. "But Callie found out something you'll want to know."

So Callie was here, which was interesting. Shannon had half expected her to have taken off for the Jonah-Dawn compound, never to be heard from again.

"Yes?" she asked as she plopped down on the only vacant chair and reached for a bagel.

"Yesterday I called one of my law-school roommates, Vera Kim." Callie's eyes shone with excitement. "She graduated ahead of me and now works in New Hampshire for the attorney general's office. I asked her to do me a favor, to research Mitchell Connor's late wife's will, and she did. It hasn't been probated yet but guess what?"

"What?"

"Joan Demeter Connor's previous will left her entire personal fortune—and there was quite a sizable one as the Demeters are an old, wealthy family—to her child, one James Demeter Connor, with his father as guardian. But four months ago, she created a new one. This final will and testament left the whole thing to—"

"JonahDawn," Shannon said, grinning. "Which dovetails perfectly with my report—I met with the great man himself last night after you left, Callie."

"Seriously?"

"He requested my presence, to see if I wanted to join his little whatever you want to call it."

Mac stopped in the act of chewing. "He what?"

Shannon nodded. "His ego is so huge, he thought he'd gotten himself another convert. Anyway, I gave him a thorough thumbs-down, then ran a couple of zingers by him to see how he responded. He was familiar with— and deeply saddened by, of course—the loss of Mitch's wife and child. So I knew that they'd been to the compound. This will thing is just icing on the cake."

"So it is," Mac said.

"There's more. This kid, Louis Lee his name is, big guy, scary. He walked me to the car, and when we got there he said, 'Is he all right?'"

She left out the threat part; again, they would worry about her.

"Is who all right?" Lupe asked.

"He didn't say, but I'm thinking he was referring to Mitch. He got freaked after he asked the question and ran away. This whole thing—Mitch's beating, his wife and child's death, it's all connected to JonahDawn, trust me."

Mac shook his head ruefully. "Which means, Counselor, your gut was on the money. You were right and I was wrong."

She waved a dismissive hand. "Let's face it. I get on my high horse and go for broke, sometimes without thinking. I need you to bring me back. Great work, Callie!" She rubbed her hands. "So now we need to fill in the blanks. I'm thinking my homeless guy, hereafter referred to by his actual name of Mitch Connor, came west to find out just what had been going on with his estranged wife and JonahDawn at the time of her death."

"And maybe even to see if they played a part in her death?" Callie added.

"Maybe even that."

Lupe muttered something in Spanish, to which Shannon replied, "Translation, please."

"Instruments of the devil."

"JonahDawn?" Mac asked.

"Yes. One of my neighbors, Loretta Florez, is fighting a foreclosure on her house because of these *diablos*. Her English isn't good and she didn't know what she was signing. I told her to come here and let us take care of it but she's scared."

"Why?"

"She thinks she might be illegal. She paid some lawyer a bunch of money years ago to get her citizenship but never heard back from him and let it slide."

"Tell her to come to see me," Shannon said. "I'll look into her citizenship for her. In fact, I'm thinking we need to gather people who have a problem with JonahDawn all across the board. Who do we have?" She counted on her fingers. "Mrs. Greenberg. Gertz and the runaway fifteen-year-old daughter. Lupe's friend who doesn't speak great English and signed over her home. A lawyer friend of mine mentioned she had an Alzheimer's patient who made Aurora her legal guardian but wasn't being taken care of properly. Maybe we can file a wrongful death action for Mitch's wife and child."

"So we're going for a civil lawsuit here or a fraud investigation?" Mac asked.

"Both. If we can find enough people who have suffered at their hypocritical hands, we can fire with both barrels. Maybe work up a class action suit—Mitch can front the suit, I'm thinking. He has the bucks."

Mac nodded. "Sounds good. Lot of work ahead of us. I'll need to call up some friends on the force. We'll need proof of actual fraud, more than we have now, to prove intent. We can't take a gut feeling that they're dirty to the D.A."

"Oh, they are," Callie piped in. "Deeply, truly dirty."

"Excuse me?" Shannon said.

"And they're really good at it. I mean, masterful. But that whole operation is as phony as a three-dollar bill."

"I was wondering if you caught on to that. Last night you sat there, looking thoroughly enthralled. Joining in on the chanting, nodding when Jonah said something he, at least, considered profound, a blissful smile on your face."

"Pure admiration," the young woman said simply. "It was a great show. See, I absolutely adored my grandfather, and he was the biggest scam artist in the world, could con anyone out of anything. My poor dad tried to follow in his footsteps, but he wasn't as gifted. He wound up in jail, and died there. It broke my mother's heart."

Mac let out a soft whistle.

"Yeah. So I can hate JonahDawn, theoretically, which I do, hate them and all they stand for. But they're good. Really good."

"Mac," Shannon said, "I believe our summer intern has larceny in her genetic makeup."

"Quite a bit of it," Callie said with a grin. "That's why I chose the law, so I wouldn't give in to my baser impulses." Her grin faded. "And I want to do all I can to bust JonahDawn from here to kingdom come."

"Good," Shannon said. "Let's assume that all their paperwork is totally legal—these folks are too slick not to have taken care of that."

"But if they follow form," Mac said, "there's another set of books or records. A shady lawyer or two on the payroll."

Shannon nodded. "I need to know how they work, need to get on the inside. How can we get someone in JonahDawn to help us?"

"You can't," Callie said. "If they're there, they're under the spell. Gone. 'Spiritual seduction,' Grandpa used to call it. So that's why I'm going in."

"Excuse me?" Shannon said.

"I thought about it since I heard from Vera. I'm perfect. Look at me. I can pass as a runaway teenager. I can do the lost-little-waif thing really well. Not to mention the fact," she said with a small smile, "that I have some youthful experience with drugs so I know how to fake the symptoms."

"Let me get this straight," Shannon said. "You want to what? Go undercover?"

"Yes."

"No."

"Why?"

"It's too dangerous. If, even minimally, what we know about them is so, they are unscrupulous and greedy. If we suspect the maximum—that they beat people up, that they're murderers!—then it's way too risky and I won't have it."

"You won't have it? Just when did I make you my mother?"

Shannon was taken aback; thus far, Callie had seemed quiet and pliable. This was a huge personality change. "I'm not your mother, I'm your boss. You worked hard to earn this internship—why do you want to throw it away?"

"Is that what I would be doing if I offer to go there for—what? Three, four days? Get vital information for an investigation? You're saying I would be giving up my internship?"

"It's a possibility."

"Do you mean that? Or are you trying to keep me from going for my own good?"

Callie was way too perceptive, darn her. "Both."

"Back to the I-don't-need-a-mother reply."

Lupe and Mac were grinning at each other. "Senoritas, please," Lupe said.

Mac followed up with "Let us use lawyerly reason here."

Temper simmering, Shannon made herself take in a breath and exhale it. Then she let go with a reluctant grin of her own. "Wow," she said to Callie. "You really do have a spine, don't you?"

"So I've been told."

She regarded the young woman. She was still not pleased with the notion of Callie entering a potentially dangerous situation. But her intern was correct— Shannon had no right to tell her what to do. And three or four days—she'd manage for that short period of time, some of which was the weekend. She had several volunteer lawyers who each gave a few hours a week. She would manage fine.

She shrugged. "Okay. I'm told I cluck too much. I withdraw all hen-like attitude. However, you can't do the innocent-waif act. Jonah knows you're my intern, probably saw you sitting with me last night."

"Shoot."

"Not to worry. I just happened to have mentioned that, while *I* sure wasn't prepared to sign on the dotted line, I thought my new intern was *eager* to enlist. He would have seen my disapproval and disappointment, neither of which were an act."

"Cool!"

"So, go to it. Just promise me you'll be careful."

"I promise. I learned how to live a double life from a master."

"I still reserve the right to worry."

It was Callie's turn to shrug. "If that's what you need to do."

Callie rose, grabbed another bagel and headed for the door. "I think I'll start my assignment this morning. I can even talk some trash about you."

"Don't get carried away," Shannon said dryly.

Mac stood, reached into his pocket and handed Callie a card. "Here's my cell phone. Memorize it, then throw it away. Call me or Shannon every day. If you get into any kind of trouble, I mean *any* kind, I'll have the cops there in two minutes. You promise me?"

"Gee, Mom and Dad," the young woman said, looking from Shannon to Mac, "I didn't know you cared. Wish me luck."

"Every day," Shannon said. "Remember that."

"If I can. Going undercover makes carrying a cell phone a bit of a problem."

"Hide it somewhere. Do it."

With a huge sigh that said she was humoring her elders, Callie said, "Okay."

"Vaya con dios," Lupe said, but as soon as the intern had left, closing the door behind her, she shook her head. "I don't like it."

"Join the club, Lupe," Shannon said, troubled as she watched Callie's retreating back.

Chapter 5

The slam of a door startled him out of his dream. He pushed himself up to a sitting position on the couch, wincing as he did because, idiot that he was, he used his sprained wrist and hand to do so.

Couch? How had he gotten to a couch? Hadn't he been on a bench at the beach? No, of course, not the beach. That was in the dream. A bed, then, he'd been in a bed.

His bed? No, the woman, the jogger—Shannon's bed. Shannon's guest bed.

A voice called out from the kitchen. "You up, Mitch?"

There was something he'd remembered, something he needed to tell her.

She came to the door of the kitchen, stood and looked at him. "Everything okay?"

He managed a nod.

"Okay, I got tacos, barbecue chicken, fried rice, salad, some grapes. A loaf of fresh French bread, sweet butter."

He shook his head; the dreams kept lingering, wanting him back in their clutches. "How many take-out places did you go to?" he managed to say, his voice gruff with sleep.

"Just one," she said with that what-the-hell grin of hers. "It's my neighborhood Tex-Mex-Chinese-salad-bar place. Don't you just love L.A.? I also have wine."

"Wine," he said, liking the sound of that. "I'd like a glass."

"You sure? You had any problems with liquor in the past? Are you on pain meds?"

"No to both."

She leveled a glare at him. "Why aren't you on pain meds?"

"Because they make me groggy and I'm already way too groggy."

"You need your rest."

He stared at her for a moment, caught halfway between mild annoyance and amusement. "Has anyone ever told you how cute you are when you get all clucky?"

Her gaze narrowed. "Not and lived through it."

"You don't like the word *cute?*"

"Hate it." Leaning her hip against the door frame, she crossed her arms under her small but perfect breasts. "Do you have any idea how hard it is to be my height? How tiring it is to live life looking up at everyone you meet? How people ruffle your hair like you're a dog? How perfect strangers smile indulgently and say, 'There, there,' when you've expressed a cogent, entirely reasonable opinion?"

"Just how short are you anyway?"

She blew out a breath, exasperated. "Did you hear anything I just said?"

"Yes. You hate being condescended to because of your height. What is it?"

"What is what?"

"Your height."

"I don't tell people."

"But you'll tell me."

"And why would I do that?"

"Because I asked."

"Oh yeah?"

"And because I've put my life in your hands. And I trust you, so you can trust me. I'm not quite sure why I do trust you, by the way, because I don't trust people, as a general rule." He shrugged. "But there it is."

She opened her eyes wide, then said, "Wow. I'm honored. Okay then. My driver's license says I'm five feet, but I'm four feet, ten and three-quarters inches."

"Not tall."

"No, not tall."

Her irritated expression made him chuckle. She tried again to glare at him; instead, she joined him with a musical chuckle of her own. It made him laugh. Actually laugh. How long had it been since he'd let loose with one of those? The air in the room lightened considerably. His dreams faded; he was back on earth.

In Shannon-land. She had the most adorable giggle. Another word she probably hated, but it was true; she was adorable and, yes, cute, although he would be very careful not to use either adjective within her hearing in the future. She was also short and curvy, with enough brains and determination for several people with several more inches on them.

He ran his tongue over his teeth. Brutal. With effort, he pushed himself up from the couch. "I need to wash my face."

"I got you a toothbrush and toothpaste. And a throw-away razor. Also another pair of clean sweats. I put it all in the bathroom. I thought you might like to shower. And no, I'm not going to assist you, not this time, anyway. I made a pact with myself to wait for the third date before bathing a man."

"My loss," he said with a chuckle. "Okay, I'm off. And when I come out I'd really like that wine."

"Coming up."

They ate on her balcony, a simple meal of wine, chicken, salad and bread. Cool evening breezes brought with them the salty smell of the nearby ocean. It was quiet and dark, lit by a single candle, and Shannon felt cosseted with Mitch in a private, intimate world.

As though he'd read her mind, Mitch said, "There's

something restful being out here with you," before adding, "even though you are not a restful person."

"Was that a compliment or a dig?"

"Neither. Just an observation."

"One I agree with. Are you warm enough?"

"Yes, Mom."

Ouch. She'd heard that one enough times today. "I only say that because being this near to the ocean, even in summertime, can get chilly at night."

"I have a beach place in Kittery," he said easily, "so I know what you mean."

"Tell me about your beach place."

As though they'd mutually agreed to take a time-out from their individual cares, Shannon found herself and Mitch chatting with the ease of old friends. She was more to the left than he was politically—which figured; he was, after all, a man of business who dealt with large amounts of money and not directly with the "little guy." She'd work on him.

He read poetry sometimes, which surprised her; she rarely sat still long enough to read much of anything except newspapers, magazines and legal briefs.

"I have a hard time relaxing," she told him.

"I noticed."

"But I actually do sometimes stretch out with a book or take a quiet walk in the woods up near Mom's place."

"But not often."

"No, not often. Too many things jumping around in my head."

"Too many wrongs to right?"

She cocked her head to one side. "Is that a bad thing?"

"No," he said thoughtfully. "The world always needs crusaders. But I've often wondered about the private lives of crusaders. If they even have one."

"Are you fishing?"

"Maybe."

She grinned. "Oh, we manage to fit in a private life here and there."

"Good to hear it."

They continued to keep it light, enjoying the quiet and the breeze and just being together. The shower had done wonders; except for the still-too-long hair, some of which kept flopping onto his forehead, Mitch looked clean and much more rested. Being with him felt, well, natural, Shannon observed.

When the meal was over, she rose. "Do you want seconds?"

He patted his stomach. "There's nowhere to put them. I can feel the pounds piling on as we speak."

"Good." She placed her plate on top of his, leaned over and pecked him on the cheek. "Back with dessert in a minute."

Shannon had been wrestling all day with whether or not she should tell him about his wife's will, maybe jog his memory. After she turned on the coffeemaker, and as she cut up fresh strawberries and pound cake, and removed the whipping cream from the freezer, she debated bringing it up again.

But he seemed relaxed, at ease, less troubled. Why should she mess with that? Even if her twenty-four-hours-a-day mind was still churning about the case, about getting back at JonahDawn for taking advantage of those who had no skills to fight their lure.

Stop, she told herself. Go back out onto the balcony, enjoy this man who has been miraculously plopped into your life…and see where it leads. Not that she had any illusions—despite that moment back at the shelter when her womb "spoke" to her. Hormones and a vivid imagination could make a pretty interesting combination.

The reality was that Mitch was extremely vulnerable right now, even if he would hate hearing that. And she was convenient. Sent to heal him. And then wave him on his way? She'd done that a few times before.

But that thought made her sad. This was different. If, or more likely, *when* they said goodbye, it would hurt.

She took a dessert plate in each hand and turned. The object of her mental meanderings stood in the doorway, for how long she had no idea.

"Oh!" she blurted out in surprise, nearly dropping the plates. He managed to reach her in time to take them from her and set them down on the counter behind her.

"Sorry," he said. "I didn't mean to scare you."

She caught her breath. "No, no, I was just thinking."

"Gotta break you of that habit," he said, standing very close, their bodies nearly touching.

"Oh," she said, surprised again, but in a much more pleasant way.

She looked up at him, studied his face, all chiseled bones and clean-shaven, his long black hair smelling of fresh shampoo, and with an inward sigh knew she was a goner. She reached up, pulled his head down, and kissed him. Really kissed him. Open mouthed, with a slow, seeking tongue. The whole deal.

He groaned, moved his body even closer so they were pressed against each other, and wrapped his arms around her. The man could kiss! She might have been the instigator, but he took right over, nibbling gently on her lips then inserting his tongue into her mouth and stroking the roof, the soft skin inside her cheeks, before dueling again with her tongue. She felt her nipples harden against his lower chest and wished she were taller. She strained on her tippy toes and he got it, because with one quick movement, he had her sitting on the counter, her legs spread, him standing between them, kissing the very life out of her.

"Wait," she said, easing her mouth away from his. "Wait a minute. This is not smart."

"Then let's be dumb." Eyes glazed with passion, he pulled her to him again.

"No, I mean, you're still healing from a pretty serious attack. Should you, you know, be doing this? Isn't it too much for you?"

He muttered a curse, released her and walked away, the fingers of his right hand raking his hair. Oh, God, had she mothered him again? Attacked his manhood in some way? She hopped down from the counter. "I'm sorry, Mitch. I didn't mean to—"

He raised his hand, waved away her apology. "No, you're right."

"I am?"

He turned around to face her. Even in the loose sweats, she could see he'd become quite aroused. She found that intensely thrilling.

"Not about my not being up to it," he said with that small, ironic smile of his. "Trust me, we'd work around it." Then the amusement left his face. "But it isn't a good idea."

"It isn't?"

He shook his head. "Me being here. You, me. Us. Kissing."

"No?"

"No."

"Why?"

"It…complicates things."

It was a fairly ambiguous, nonspecific answer, and Shannon was about to ask for a more thorough explanation, when her gut told her to shut up. Not to push the man, not to require any more of him tonight than he wanted to give her. Which annoyed her, even though she knew she would do as instructed.

The smell of freshly brewed coffee filled the kitchen. She retrieved the dessert plates, held them out. "Okay," she said cheerfully. "Let's table that discussion for another time."

"Table it," he repeated, amused by her again. Then—and did she catch a fleeting glimpse of regret?—he said, "Probably the smart thing to do."

"You take the plates and I'll bring the coffee. Meet you on the balcony in five minutes."

After which, she would eat her dessert, drink some coffee and head to bed. Alone.

But she would replay this evening, after she was under the covers. She would remember the feel of his body against hers, the way her nipples had hardened and her skin had heated up, how she'd grown soft and moist between her legs, all in the space of seconds. Oh yes, she'd remember.

She had a feeling Mitch Connor would remember it, too.

"You want the business section?" Shannon asked the next morning.

She was sprawled on her favorite armchair and ottoman, happily surrounded by sections of her customary Sunday reading, both the *New York* and *L.A. Times*, her Nordstrom, Bloomingdale's and RedEnvelope catalogs, and a couple of entertainment gossip magazines that she always saved for last—guilty pleasures that required discipline or she'd get lost in them and never get anything else done.

At his pretty emphatic "No," she glanced over at

Mitch, seated on her couch, studying the news section of one of the papers.

"Really? You don't want to know what's up with the world of finance? Maybe even your very own business?"

"No," he said again, but didn't elucidate.

Hmm, she thought, wondering what that was about. Aversion? Fear? Denial? Disinterest? All of the above?

"Okay, then. How about the Sunday *Style* section?"

"Do you actually read that thing?"

She grinned. "Are you kidding? With all the little stories about how the happy couple met and where the wedding reception was held, and who daddy and mommy and step-mommy and step-daddy are? Sure. It's fun."

"If you like nightmares."

"Let me take a wild guess. You and your wife were written up in there."

"We sure were," he said dryly. "Not my kind of thing. Being invaded, insisting on all the details about that magic moment when we first 'knew.'" He shook his head. "But Joan loved it, it made her happy." With that, he shrugged and went back to whatever story he was reading.

She wondered how she could get him to talk more about Joan, about his marriage. She sure was curious.

"More coffee, then?" Shannon said, pushing at least a small tree's worth of byproduct off her lap and rising, grabbing her cup and heading for the kitchen.

"No, thanks."

What was up with him this morning? she wondered. He wasn't exactly grumpy, but not really present. Kind of distant, distracted. Had the kitchen encounter last night affected him so deeply that he was trying to push her away? No, that wasn't the vibe she was picking up. Let it go, she told herself. Mitch was allowed to be in whatever kind of mood he wanted to be.

Still, after she poured herself another cup of coffee, debating if yet one more muffin top—raspberry-bran this time—was called for, she stood in the doorway of the kitchen and gazed at her houseguest, his head lowered as he read the paper, spread out on the coffee table for ease of turning with his one good hand. No bald spot on the top of his head, she thought distractedly. Nice sign. Usually by his age if a man was going to lose his hair, there would be some scalp beginning to show through. No, he had nice thick black hair, shot through with silver. Not gray, but a true silver that picked up glints from the sun streaming in through her high windows.

If the sun was streaming in, then it must be nearly noon, she figured, and glanced back at the kitchen wall clock. Eleven-forty-five, as a matter of fact.

They could sit around all day, she supposed, continuing this same non-communication, but comfortable enough. *She* was comfortable, at least; she couldn't vouch for him. Or she was mostly comfortable.

And yeah, tired. As she'd predicted, she'd tossed and turned most of the night, thinking of the man in the next bedroom. He really did have a lot of baggage, at the moment for sure—he was in mourning, recovering his health; there were still parts of his recent life he couldn't remember. She *needed* him to remember, so they could talk about him fronting the suit, about his wife's will, little details like that, having to do with JonahDawn.

JonahDawn. The compound on the mountaintop. At this moment, Callie was up there. It was already noon and Shannon hadn't heard from her yet. Hurriedly she darted back into the kitchen where her cell phone was charging on the counter, picked it up and speed-dialed Mac.

Before she got out a greeting, he beat her to it. "Tell me you've heard from her."

"Just about to ask you the same thing. No."

"Damn," he muttered. "Then tell me again why we let her do this?"

"We didn't let her do anything, remember? She made all the decisions. Next time I get an intern, remind me to get it in writing that they do nothing but stay chained to their desk, 24-7, looking up legal precedents."

"Got it."

"Well, look, it's a beautiful day, let's think positive thoughts."

"You think whatever kind of thoughts you like, Shannon," he muttered. "I'm gonna keep worrying."

"Then we have all our bases covered."

When she walked out of the kitchen, Mitch looked up from his reading. "Everything okay?"

"Sure," she said, trying for casual. "Just some office stuff."

Maybe she ought to tell him what was up, which would mean bringing him up to speed on the whole JonahDawn/will thing. Again, she asked herself if she should ruin a perfectly lovely Sunday morning by reminding him of his loss.

Resuming her former position in the kitchen doorway, she gazed at the definitely non-balding, mostly black-haired top of Mitchell Connor's head, her thoughts straying away from Callie and back to herself.

She would like to marry someday. If she could find a man who could keep up with her brain and her energy, who wasn't threatened by her nosiness, her natural assertiveness, who liked really short women with curly hair that refused to be tamed no matter what, slightly thick thighs and not-large breasts. The men were out there, or so she'd been told.

Was Mitchell Connor a candidate? she wondered idly. "Hmm."

She wasn't aware she'd said it out loud until the object of her perusal glanced up at her, a question in his eyes. "Sure you're okay?" he asked.

"Just fine," she bluffed. "Hey, it's nearly noon!"

"And that's a bad thing?" His smile said he found her vastly entertaining.

Being thought of with amusement usually pissed

her off but in his case it didn't, because she knew he wasn't laughing *at* her, or disapproving *of* her; he was just…letting her be. Enjoying who she was.

Hmm, she mused again, silently this time. How did he stand on the subject of chunky thighs?

"You up for a movie?" she found herself saying.

He considered this. "What kind?"

"Personally, I like small, independent films, preferably with subtitles. How do you feel about Chinese?"

"Movies or food?"

"Both. There's a great new Gong Li and a really good Mandarin place about ten minutes from here."

"You're on." He pushed himself up from the couch, his movements stiff but willing.

"You can sit that long?"

"I'll take a half a pain pill."

"You can walk from the parking lot to the movie?"

"I don't really need the cane but I'll bring it along. Anything else you need to know, before I can go out to play?"

She made a face. "Busted. Again. Sorry."

"It's okay. It's even a little—" he shrugged "—comforting. Once in a while, anyway."

"Really?"

"Really." More serious now, he added, "But I need you to remember that I am a grown-up, Shannon. I long ago stopped needing anyone to take care of me or to run my life."

"Gotcha."

* * *

She was a whiz with chopsticks, Mitch noticed, and she ate with gusto, none of that picking at her food, leaving most of it on the plate, the way Joan had. Joan, who had been terrified of getting fat, who had been ter-rified of the dark, who had been terrified of so many things that he should have paid more attention along the way to the signs.

He tried to brush it away. Didn't he deserve time off from the guilt and self-recrimination? They'd been gnawing at him for days; today they'd been particu-larly powerful, which must have made him pretty sorry company.

Here he was at a decent restaurant, having seen an entertaining film, sitting across from a woman who was the diametrical opposite of Joan. His late wife had been tall and willowy and quiet and phobic. None of those adjectives applied to Shannon Coyle. If she had a fear in her body, he'd yet to see a hint of it.

"I enjoyed the movie," he said. "It got my mind off myself."

"They really know how to do the whole ninja, flying thing, don't they? And those colors. Amazing, huh?"

"Amazing," he agreed. "I've always wanted to go to China."

"Yeah, me, too." She grinned. "Well, life's not over yet, so maybe we'll both get to go."

She would be fun to travel with. He wouldn't have to worry about her all the time, wouldn't have her

clinging to him every time something came up that was
in the least bit different from what had been planned.
She would adapt, adjust, make it a game.

Shannon was just plain fun. How long had it been
since he'd had fun? A long time, even before Jamie's
death.

Help me, Daddy.

He lowered his head, so she wouldn't see his face.
Please, Jamie, he begged the voice, all the voices that
came out of the blackness. Please let me have a break.

And what was it he'd remembered yesterday that
he'd wanted to tell Shannon? It just wouldn't come.

"Talk to me about yourself," he said, needing to
move his attention off himself. "If you don't mind."

"It's not a very interesting story."

"I doubt that."

"Trust me." She grinned at him. "I'm the oldest of
three. My younger sister, Carmen—well, Goldie,
legally, but she prefers Carmen—she got married last
year to J.R., one of my oldest friends, and she's expecting. Oh, I was supposed to call her. Darn. Anyway,
she's into plants, big time. The greenest thumb ever.
And our baby brother, Shane, just got back from a fel-
lowship at Oxford. One-upping his big sister's perfectly respectable credentials from UCLA undergrad,
followed by Boalt Law at UC Berkeley, and thus continuing our always-friendly rivalry. Mom's a psychologist, Dad was a professor. He died a few years back and
I miss him dreadfully."

Her love for her family shone through every word, every gesture; that warmth of hers drew you in, made you want to be part of her world. Not to mention how her rounded body in today's body-hugging sweater and faded jeans also drew him. Warmth, softness and curves on a woman who seemed to accept herself, to like herself. What a concept.

"Anyhow," she was saying, "we're all very close. That day I found you lying in front of the Last House on the Block, I'd just gotten back from a big family celebration welcoming the young idiot home."

"The Last House on the Block?"

"That's the name of my storefront—it's a saying from the twelve-step programs. It means when you have nowhere else to go, no one else to turn to, you have to come to us. We're your last chance."

"For what, exactly?"

"Justice, pretty much. Victims of unfair contracts, real-estate scams, child-custody battles, landlord abuse, job harassment. We're there for those who need legal help and can't afford to pay for it."

"That covers a hell of a lot of people."

"I try to pick my battles. I can't save the entire world, but I can make a little bit of a difference." She shrugged. "Or so I tell myself."

"Why?"

"Why what?"

"Why are you that way?"

"I have no idea. I just always have been. And no, I

don't have a sordid backstory to explain it, no childhood deprivation or the family getting screwed by unscrupulous land developers. I was just—" she shrugged "—born this way."

"I've always wondered how it might feel to be part of a close family."

"Not your experience, huh?"

"No. Not my experience," he said, picking up his chopsticks.

"I'm lucky, I know I am. So?"

He looked up. "So, what?"

She pushed her plate away, patted her mouth with a napkin. "Your turn."

When he grimaced with displeasure, she insisted. "Hey, it's only fair."

"You know most of it already."

"Cop-out."

"Okay, okay," he found himself saying good-naturedly, but determined not to dwell too long on himself. "I'm a classic up-from-poor story. Only child, mom sick a lot, died of cancer when I was twelve. Dad worked as a day laborer after the unions went bust. I got into a little trouble as a teenager, got lucky with a counselor who decided I had brains, managed to get a scholarship to BU. I thought I wanted law, found I had a talent for business instead."

"How did you meet Joan? Do you mind talking about her?"

"No, it's okay. I met her at a party, we dated for a

year and then we married. She opened up social doors for me—not that I married her because of that, by the way. Just in case you were thinking it."

"It hadn't crossed my mind."

But it had crossed his, many times over the years, and each time, disgusted with himself, he'd pushed it away and tried even harder to be a better husband. He took a sip of his tea, mused briefly on the pattern of his wrongdoings. He'd lived a self-centered life, motivated by ambition, the need to prove himself, to the exclusion of everything else.

"When did your dad die?"

"About four years ago. There was a fire. He left a cigarette burning and fell asleep."

"Wow, that's tough."

"We weren't close, but yeah. At least he got to see Jamie. Joan and I were married for seven years before Jamie was born. The business expanded some more." He shrugged. "That's it."

"Work, work, work."

"Which is why I never got to China."

She nodded. "Me, too."

A buzzing noise interrupted the moment; Shannon was sorry that it had. She looked around for her purse, then dug into it and produced her cell phone. She'd set it to vibrate during the movie and forgotten to turn it back on. "Hello?"

"She called me." It was Mac's bass rumble on the line.

"Tell me."

"She's in, everything's fine, Jonah is crowing about his triumph over you, she's shaved her head."

"She what?"

"It's part of the initiation ritual."

Shannon buried her face in her hand. "I really don't like this, Mac."

"You think I'm dancin' around the room here? I'm thinking about heading over to the compound and hauling her bony ass out of there."

"But you can't. I mean, you have no legal right."

"Can't you come up with something? Like how she's in a weakened mental state?"

"From what? Studying for the bar?" She sighed, shook her head, having regret upon regret upon regret. "Look, Mac, maybe it'll be okay. Maybe she'll find out some stuff for us."

"And maybe we'll have another drowning victim."

That one chilled her to the bone. "Don't, Mac. Please."

She heard him hiss in a breath then push it out. "Okay, okay. Sorry. I'm feeling like one of my kids has run off to the Middle East because she heard that's where all the fun parties are."

"I know. Did she say anything else?"

"Nope. It was quick, whispered, and I've told you all of it."

"She's a clever girl, Mac. We need to give her some space."

"Still don't like it," he said again.

"I hear you. See you tomorrow morning."

After she disconnected, Mitch was looking at her with interest. "That was one of my work associates," she told him.

"You sound worried."

"We kind of are. I have this intern working for me this summer. Callie Kennedy. You met her. The one who looks about twelve? She's doing a little…undercover work. And she's, well, she's undercover. We're worried about her."

At that moment, the waiter placed the bill on the table. Shannon looked at it and threw some bills on the table, then rose. "Shall we?"

"You're keeping tabs on how much all of this is costing, right?"

"Sure. And now that I know you're wealthy, I'll try not to pad the expenses," she added with a grin, "but it won't be easy. You up for a little drive?"

Playa del Rey was yet one more California dichotomy among so many others. Built on a series of hills overlooking the Pacific, the vegetation was lush and green, the homes nestled among them spacious, the ocean views breathtaking…and the airport was a mile away. So residents got everything anyone could want of the famous Southern California way of life, accompanied by constant noise from jets flying overhead all day long.

The JonahDawn compound was in Playa del Rey,

and Shannon's purpose for driving there was twofold—not only to see if she could get a glimpse of a bald-headed and—please God—breathing Callie, but maybe to shake Mitch's memory a little about his three missing months.

As the last of the day's sun disappeared, she headed up a winding side road, past a park and then some more homes, until a tall gate made of iron bars came into view. She backed her car into a nearby break in the bushes, so their presence wouldn't be picked up by the security cameras, turned off the lights and engine, and stared.

There was a full moon tonight, casting its glow on the scene: Beyond the gate, about fifty yards further on, stood what could only be described as a small castle, complete with balconies and turrets, its silhouette in shadow against the evening sky. The only thing missing was a moat and drawbridge, and Shannon had no doubt that if Jonah Denton could create one, he would. The compound had, up until four years ago, been the private retreat of some dot-com billionaire who had gone bust. The JonahDawn folks had picked it up in a foreclosure sale, at a bargain price, which in the L.A. area was still certainly in the several millions.

No one was in sight, Shannon observed with disappointment. Which meant Callie was inside, one of many shaved heads, her eyes shining with the light of the true believer, counterfeit-style. Was Jonah being taken in, or was the con man—despite his mountainous ego—

adept at filtering out others like him, those who came off to most of the world as sincere and trustworthy, while picking their pockets?

She glanced to her right to see if Mitch was having any kind of reaction. He was. Frowning, he stared straight ahead, an aura of uneasy energy surrounding him.

"What is it, Mitch?" She tried to keep her voice gently inquiring.

He was aware of Shannon's question, but only vaguely. The black was back, a throbbing, pulsating darkness that filled his head and blocked out everything else. Or almost everything.

This place he was staring at. It was evil. It had taken his child and Joan because... Damn it, because what? What was the thing he needed to tell Shannon?

The will.

Yes. Now he remembered what he'd discovered in yesterday's dream but had not been able to recall later on. The will. When he'd found out about the will, it had turned things all around. He'd known then. Known for sure. His jaw clenched with anger.

"Mitch?" Again Shannon's voice broke the darkness, stronger this time. He felt her hand on his arm. "Are you all right?"

He gave a quick nod, but didn't speak.

"Are you remembering?"

He had to swallow before answering, his voice a hoarse whisper. "They killed Jamie and Joan."

"Who?"

"Them." He thrust his chin at the castle. "JonahDawn."

"How do you know?" she asked, repressed excitement in her voice.

"The will. She left it all to them. Those bastards killed my family."

The anger grew, becoming full-blown rage. He needed to get to them, to take his revenge on these evil child-killers, make them pay.

He reached for the car door handle, but her voice stopped him. "No. Don't. Please."

The sound was like a faint warning bell breaking through a furious thunderstorm. He stilled his movements, looked over at her.

Earnest large brown eyes shone in the moonlight. Small face, curls all around, untamed like her energy. "Don't, Mitch. We'll get them. Talk to me instead. Tell me what you remember."

He looked back up at the evil place. The black rage filled his head again. He shook it, tried to push the blackness away.

"Not here," he said gruffly. "Let's get the hell away from here."

Chapter 6

The ride back to Shannon's took place in silence, which with the part of his brain that was still functioning, amazed him. She was actually not talking, not peppering him with questions, for which he was grateful. Mitch's insides were churning; having his memory returned to him was proving to be more punishment than revelation. He'd made so many poor, selfish choices along the way, choices that had ended up costing those precious to him their lives. Tonight, the weight of anger and self-recrimination he'd been feeling all day was close to crushing him.

Once back at her condo, his instinct was to head for his room and close the door, to try to block out the memories. But he didn't think he'd be successful at hiding, not tonight, so instead he lowered himself onto the couch. His body was aching, all over, to add to the churning emotions inside him. He made himself breathe deeply, willing his boiling blood to cool down. He watched Shannon put a log in the fireplace and get a blaze started, then bustle around in the kitchen and come back with a pot of tea, cups and a plate of cookies, oatmeal this time.

"Are there any cookies or muffins you don't like?" he asked, trying for some kind of human normalcy.

"Nope," she said with a grin. "And I'm carrying about ten pounds to prove it."

"I like it," he said, meaning it. "Most women really fuss over their weight. Does it bother you?"

"It used to. No more. Life's too short. So, tell me what went on back there. What you couldn't talk about."

Ah, she was back. Shannon of the multiple questions.

He closed his eyes, rested his head against the couch's comfortable cushion. He was exhausted and heart sore and sick to death of being him.

Several moments of silence went by before she said, softly, "It will make the healing go faster if you do, you know."

When he opened his eyes, it was to see her sitting on the floor on the other side of the coffee table, her arms wrapped around her bent knees, a large cup in her hand. "Or are you the brooding type? One of those men who can't tolerate talking about whatever is going on inside? Who lets it sit in there, eat at them, make them lose sleep? Or maybe work it out with furious exercise or driving way too fast or some killer drugs?"

Despite the heaviness in his heart, he couldn't help smiling. "It's amazing how you reduce one half of the human race to a stereotype."

"Women can be just as bad—I'm an equal-opportunity stereotyper," she said with a trace of her former cheer. "But seriously. Something happened to you back there when we were looking at the castle."

He nodded. "I remembered. All of it. The missing pieces."

To her credit, she didn't say a thing, just waited.

And he knew there really wasn't any choice. He would tell her. For some unfathomable reason, Shannon Coyle made him want to talk to her. About himself. About Jamie. About all of it. After a lifetime of, yes, being one of those mostly silent, non-sharing men she had just described in her usual colorful and indignant terms, he would break that pattern tonight.

No one had ever had this effect on him. No one.

"It was about a month before they died," he began. "I'd had Jamie for the weekend and when I brought him back to Joan on that Sunday night, she was packing up some suitcases, his and hers. I asked her what she was doing, and she announced that she was taking him with her out to California for a while. I told her she couldn't take him anywhere without my permission and I wanted more details. She went on about being in contact with this group, this JonahDawn. She'd mentioned them before a couple of times—she was always going off half-cocked about finding the meaning in life. It was her search for God. She'd been raised in the Episcopal church and had taken it all quite seriously, but then she'd broken away from them and it had left some kind of void in her. So I wasn't concerned, not really, at first. I mean, she was allowed a spiritual quest—hell, mankind's been on that journey since Adam and Eve."

"Got it."

"But this time, I don't know, she sounded different. Kind of manic and serene at the same time. There was a look in her eye that felt…off somehow. You know? Secretive. Like she was having visions or hearing voices but not telling me about them. And I remembered back to a few other times, when she'd acted, I don't know, not quite right. Not quite like Joan. She'd always been, not cold, but remote. Quiet.

"In the beginning, it was attractive. You wanted to find out what was behind all that quiet, sure that there were mysterious, interesting, complex thoughts going on. And she was beautiful, I admit it, and I liked having her on my arm. And she wanted to be with me, even though her family disapproved. They were *Mayflower* descendents, and snobby as hell, and I was up from second-generation Scotch-Irish factory workers. I was flattered, my ego was stroked that she thought me worth the fight."

He shook his head at his folly. "Later on I realized I'd been an excuse to break away from her family. That she didn't have the backbone to stand on her own, so she did it through me. That behind that mysterious quiet was a shy and depressed woman in need of therapy or meds, something. Incidentally, she was a wonderful mother, absolutely adored Jamie and he adored her."

"I'm so glad." Shannon smiled at him, encouraging him.

His mouth was dry so he took a sip of his tea; it felt soothing. "I tried to get her to seek some help, but she refused, said she would be fine as soon as she found her god place. That was what she called it, her 'god place.' I was pretty cynical about that kind of thing, but I wanted to be fair." He scrubbed at his face with his good hand. "The marriage was a mistake from the start but we stuck it out for twelve years. Denial is an amazing thing. I was busy building my empire and barely had time to deal with my home life. Twelve lonely years," he said thoughtfully, "eight until Jamie was born, and four more afterward, until we faced each other one day and agreed that it was over. There was no rancor, not really. It was just…dead."

"That was a year ago?"

"Yes."

"So what happened that day when she said she was going to California?"

"I wondered if she was becoming mentally ill. And in the back of my mind I debated whether or not to do something to stop her from going. But she smiled and said everything was fine. Jamie was fine, she was fine, she was just continuing her search and they'd be home in a couple of weeks. That she just had to check this out, in person. This JonahDawn."

His body felt stiff and sore; he sat straighter, rested his elbows on his knees, rotated his head to loosen up his neck.

"You okay?"

"Sure." He made himself go on. "I was in the middle of this merger and was distracted. Even so, I suggested she leave Jamie with me while she went to the coast, that I would feel better if she did that. She ran into his room, where he was playing, picked him up and said, 'Jamie, Mommy has to go away and Daddy wants you to stay with him while I do.' He screamed 'No, no!' with his arms around Joan's neck. 'No, Daddy, I want to stay with Mommy.' With tears streaming down his face."

Shannon could picture the scene all too well and had an instant of intense dislike of Joan Connor for being manipulative. Using a child's tender sensibilities to win an argument against his father. That sucked.

Mitch must have noticed the expression of disapproval on her face because he nodded. "I knew she was working me, she'd gotten pretty good at that, but—" again, he shrugged "—hey, I couldn't get past my little boy's tears." He closed his eyes, leaned his head against the back of the couch. "And so I let them go. I let my business decide for me. I saw the signs of mental illness, my gut was telling me something was wrong, and I let my son go with her, off to his death."

"You couldn't have known."

"Yeah, I could have," he said bitterly. "Someone paying attention on the home front would have known what to do. Take the little boy from his mother, screaming and crying or not, call the lawyer, let Joan get on with her journey but not with my son. Not with my son. But I didn't."

He seemed to go inside himself then. Shannon watched his face, hurting for him, the silence in the room broken only by the sound of the crackling fire.

After a while he sat up again, took a sip of his tea, went on with the story. "I made a mental note to deal with all of this after my European trip and the merger. Only a couple of weeks, I told myself. And Joan was such a wonderful mother, no matter her state of mind, that nothing would happen to Jamie, nothing. I talked to them two or three times a week and he sounded fine, happy even. There were other children and it was so nice there. It was a huge castle, just like in the books we read to him. And they went to the ocean a lot and he played in the sand. And I thought it would be all right.

"Until the day I got the phone call. I was in the middle of a meeting when my cell phone rang. I excused myself for a moment. It was Jamie. 'Help me, Daddy,' he said. 'And Mommy, too. Help us.'"

"Oh, no." Shannon spoke aloud, her heart wrenched

with pain for that poor little boy and for the man who sat before her, agony carved on his face like an ancient death mask.

"'Help me, Daddy,'" Mitch repeated, his voice hollow. "I think I'll be hearing that on my death bed."

A breeze blew in from the open balcony door, making the fireplace flames flicker, casting dancing shadows on the far wall. But her attention was riveted to the man seated on the couch. She waited for him to speak, because there was more to tell, but it was his timetable, not hers.

And finally he did. "I heard a man's voice saying, 'Gimme that,' and then we got disconnected. Needless to say, I was frantic. I canceled my meetings, tried Joan's cell. Nothing. Called my secretary in New Hampshire and told her to contact JonahDawn. I called the police in California, but they said there was too little to go on. I called a private security firm, got them on it. I felt absolutely insane during the flight back. Pacing up and down the aisles the entire time, a bad feeling in my gut. A really bad feeling. Kicking myself, hating myself.

"For good reason. By the time I arrived at JFK, I was told there was no trace of them. The security firm had been to the JonahDawn compound, and they said Joan and Jamie had taken off the day before for a picnic. No one had seen them since. Their luggage was still there. The cops were searching for them."

Again he paused, his eyes dry but his expression one

of a man crying inside. He swallowed before saying, "I got on a plane for California. That night, they found the bodies, down the coast about fifty miles or so. I had just landed when I got the news. A drowning accident. There was still some picnic stuff in a small boat Joan had rented. She'd always sailed, she was a fine sailor. But that didn't make a difference. No one knew what had happened, no eyewitnesses, just two bodies.

"And as I heard the news, something inside me died. I knew I would never recover from this, would never forgive myself. Never."

Shannon rose from the floor, set her untouched mug of tea on the coffee table and took a seat next to Mitch on the couch. His unbandaged hand rested limply on his lap; she lifted it, took it between both of hers. It was so cold. She held it tight, her eyes brimming. She understood the pain in his eyes now. God, how could she not?

"Oh, Mitch, how awful for you," she murmured.

He stared into the fireplace for a long time before continuing. "Death by drowning. An accident. That's what the autopsy report said. I brought the bodies home and we had the funeral. That awful funeral with Joan's casket and my son's side by side." He turned to face her. "Do you have any idea how that felt? No, how could you?"

"You're right. I have no idea."

His gaze returned to the fireplace for a while longer before he shook his head, as though trying to clear it. "Afterward, a lawyer in California contacted me about a new will Joan had made. It surprised me. I didn't care about the money—I have enough for several life-times—but I took it as one more piece of proof that Joan had gone over the edge into true mental illness. I mean, leaving your fortune to a bunch of phonies."

"Did you know they were phonies? Had you investigated them?"

"No, I hadn't. Too busy," he said with disgust. "But call it a healthy suspicion of any group of people who have declared themselves in possession of the One Truth, who chant and shave their heads, who live in a castle in—pardon me—California, of all places."

Despite the seriousness of the conversation, the quintessential easterner's contempt for all things west coast made her smile. "We're the home of the nuts and the fruits, for sure. But hey, we're not so bad once you get to know us."

"Yeah, well, whatever. In New England you're viewed with suspicion, all of you, with your health food and sunshine and celebrities and Hummers. It doesn't seem real."

"I know," she said, thinking they'd have a discussion about this one day, in which she would set him straight about the *real* California, the land of innovation and creative freedom…alongside the nuts and the fruits and the cults. "Go on."

"Anyway, I told my second in command to take over the merger discussions, that I had to get away for a while. Everyone was very nice about it. Everyone understood. I took a lot of money out of my bank account. I don't know, maybe I knew I wanted to just get lost, for no one to be able to find me, not to be traceable by using my credit card. I wasn't thinking real clearly. I got in my car and began to drive. I wandered, stayed at cheap motels, paid for everything with cash. Sometimes I drank too much to forget but the next day I still remembered, and on top of it I felt like crap. I honestly have no idea where I went.

"At one point my car developed engine trouble. I just left it, wherever I was, somewhere in Wyoming, I think. I traveled by train, bus, hitched a few times. What I know now is that I was on my way out to the coast, that something was bothering me. Apart from the guilt I mean. It kept…yammering at me. I dismissed it, the way I did my notice of Joan's mental deterioration, but it kept at me. Something was wrong, something having to do with their deaths."

Shifting his position slightly, he turned to make eye contact with her. "Joan was a wonderful sailor and she would never have allowed Jamie to get into a boat without a life vest. Never. But he didn't have one on when they found him. She was also a fine swimmer, strong. Why would she just drown? It didn't make sense. Oh, sure, there was mention of suicide and several people said she'd been kind of unstable lately so it was certainly possible. For Joan, maybe. But taking Jamie with her? Sacrificing him? Never. And then there was the will. Leaving her estate—as I said she was from old stock and there were trust funds, plenty of money involved—to these people, well, let's just say, JonahDawn got a major windfall."

"I'll bet they did."

"Anyhow, it just smelled bad. I got to a library and did some research, read some newspaper articles. Did as much of a background check as I could, but I found nothing criminal. JonahDawn paid their taxes, were good neighbors. They had a following, not huge, but loyal, and definitely growing. If there were any lawsuits filed against them, I didn't find them."

"It never gets that far," Shannon said. "They prefer to settle—don't want any bad publicity."

He nodded. "Which explains why, on the surface, I could find nothing. They even seemed to be quite generous, a soup kitchen for the homeless, one of the sponsors of a 10k walk to fight breast cancer. I began to wonder if maybe I was covering up my guilt by trying to place blame somewhere other than on myself. I knew I needed to do something, I just didn't know what. I couldn't just barge in there and demand to know what they'd done to my wife and child, even if part of me wanted to.

"And then, I don't know, one day I looked in the mirror and saw that I hadn't shaved or had a haircut in weeks, that I'd lost fifteen or twenty pounds, and I looked, well, like I was wasting away. And that I didn't care. Which is when it came to me what I would do— I would pose as a homeless person, get as close to them as I could, see what I could find."

Shannon nodded. "Smart move. It's funny how invisible the homeless seem to us. We never take the time to see that there's a real person underneath, with a life story and a family who might have once loved him."

That got a small smile from him. "One of your pet injustices, I'm thinking."

"Got me. Sorry. Go on."

"You're right, though. That was my reasoning. I would fade into the woodwork most of the time. I'd look harmless, hang around, talk to people, see if I could find something, some *proof*. It was insane, really, I mean, playing detective, pretending to be someone I wasn't."

"You weren't afraid they'd recognize you?"

"No. I never did meet any of them, that time I went to claim the bodies. I'd never been up to the castle, not at that point. I looked nothing like any pictures of me they might have seen, trust me." He shrugged. "Mostly, I decided I had nothing to lose. That if I died trying to find out, I really didn't care. And that's the truth."

The eyes again, a dull silver, bleak and hopeless. It made her wonder if he still felt that way.

"And so I did it. Got myself to California, found out where Playa del Rey was, took a bus, hung around near the beach for a few days, didn't shower, got sand under my fingernails, got to looking even more ragged. And then I walked up that hill on soup-kitchen day, and basically never left. They told me to go away. I pretended to be not all there mentally, asked if I could work for food and a place to sleep. Someone took pity on me, fed me. I began hanging around pretty much every day, got to know a few of the acolytes."

A sad shake of the head was followed by "Young kids mostly, runaways with awful childhoods. Learning disabilities, incest and abuse victims. A few recovering alcoholics and drug addicts who swore they'd been miraculously cured by JonahDawn. Even some young families, moms, dads, kids, all with that look in their eyes. The light of the true believer," he added with disgust. "It reminded me of some newsreel footage from that mass suicide way back when we were kids. Jim Jones and Jonestown. Remember that?"

She nodded. "In the late seventies. We studied it in a sociology class I took in college. Over 900 of them took poison because he ordered them to. They called him 'Father,' just like they do Jonah." She shuddered. "Awful."

"There was one young man, Louis, big, not quite right in the head. He followed Jonah and Aurora like a loyal dog. He had that look in his eyes, too."

"I met him recently. Yeah. That glassy look."

"When did you meet him?"

"Callie and I went to one of their public meetings the other night."

"Oh."

A popping sound from the fireplace made them both start with surprise. A piece of the log had broken off and rolled toward the screen. Shannon began to get up but Mitch said, "Let me."

Bringing her legs up onto the couch and folding

them to one side, she watched Mitch take the poker and push the piece of wood back toward the grate. After he put the poker back with the other tools, he remained standing, staring at the fire.

"So, did you find anything at the compound?" she prompted.

He turned to face her, propping a shoulder against the mantel. He was so tall, she thought. And lean. And haunted.

"Not at first. I snuck around a lot, looked in closets. Their office was always locked, and to all appearances they didn't live high on the hog. There was plain food, plain clothing, not poverty level, but nothing materialistic. Their bedroom door was locked also, but one day I managed to sneak in to have a look around." He shook his head. "And I swear, Shannon, it was like a cross between a sultan's harem and the cover of *Architectural Digest*. It was huge, three, four times the size of your living room, and everything was of the highest, most expensive, gaudiest quality. Hanging silks, antiques, a state-of-the-art TV and sound system. Silver and gold everywhere, a huge bed, covered in fur. Real fur."

Shannon's mouth dropped open. "You're serious?"

"Even a mirrored ceiling. Like some Las Vegas bordello."

"No!"

"Yes." He raised his hand, palm to her. "Now, ordinarily I don't give a damn how people live their lives in private, but this just smelled to high heaven. There was such a…disconnect between how everyone else on the compound lived—so simple, Spartan, even—and the Dentons' secret, *voluptuous* life behind those doors. I heard someone coming and lay down on the bed and pretended I'd fallen asleep there. And then—" he shook his head "—it gets vague."

"Tell me the last thing you do remember."

"Louis. Well, you met him so you know. He's a kid, really, but big, threatening-looking. He was always telling me to get off the property then apologizing when he did. Orders, he would say. I think he may have been the one who found me that day on the bed, but I'm not sure. I know I got tossed off the property. I remember walking away, feeling discouraged."

"I'm pretty sure Louis is the one who beat you up."

He nodded. "I wouldn't be surprised. He's their enforcer."

Shannon let the silence that followed last for another long moment before asking gently, "And that's it?"

"I have no memory after that until waking up in the hospital."

She nodded, rose. "And you may never remember."

She gathered their cups and headed for the kitchen. Mitch followed her.

"When I was nine," she said, "I was riding my bike and a car hit me, and from what everyone tells me, I was bleeding all over the road from my head and they were sure I would die. I was rushed to the emergency room and they had to operate on a blood clot that had formed in my brain. My mom and dad and Carmen went nuts because they thought either that I would have brain damage or that they were going to lose me."

"Wow."

"They didn't lose me, needless to say," she added with a rueful smile, "and if I have a damaged brain, ah well, it hasn't slowed me down. More tea?"

"No thanks."

She turned the kettle back on to boil for her second cup, then stood leaning against the counter. "And the thing is, all I remember about that day was getting up that morning and looking out the window and deciding it would be a great day to ride my bike." She shrugged. "What is that—twenty-four, twenty-five years ago? And I still can't remember a thing about the accident."

He stood in the doorway, obviously listening to her but also somewhere in his head. His jaw looked tense; his posture was most definitely not relaxed. She'd thought—hoped—that getting it all out would help. Or had it made it worse? She couldn't tell.

She had a sudden flash of the two of them being in this same room and in similar positions just last night. Then the mood had been all sensuality and hunger. Tonight, a heavy sadness permeated the atmosphere. Mitch's basic nature, from what she could tell, was that of a boss—aggressive, strong and decisive. Standing before her, he was the opposite; there was about him an air of hopelessness, of being lost. It had to be throwing him, big time. She hoped, for his sake, that it wouldn't last too long.

She smiled encouragingly. "Hey, at least you now remember everything, right? You have your entire memory back, except for the day of the beating?"

He took a moment to consider, then nodded. "So it seems. Yes."

"And we still come back to JonahDawn."

"Yes." His fingers clenched and unclenched. "I still have nothing concrete, but I'm positive they had a hand in Joan and Jamie's deaths. The will, the timing. It's too much of a coincidence."

"I agree."

Suddenly he winced, closed his eyes tight.

She moved to him. "What is it, Mitch?"

"A horrible headache. And the voice again. Jamie's voice. *'Help me, Daddy.'*" He fisted his unbandaged hand against the side of his head. "God, will it ever stop?" He took his fist and banged it against the door frame. Once, twice, three times, his face contorted now not with pain but with rage.

She was momentarily taken aback by the intensity of his anger. "Mitch?" He didn't answer. "It'll be okay," she said and even as she did she realized how lame it sounded.

"No it won't," he told her fiercely. "It will never be okay."

She reached a hand out toward him. "Mitch?"

"Don't." The demand was sharp and brooked no discussion.

Whirling around, he headed out to the balcony, closing the sliding glass door behind him, and stood there, staring out at the darkness. A cloud cover had come up to hide the moon and stars. She watched his back, rigid and unforgiving, and she hurt for him.

The urge to comfort was strong; she wanted to run out there, to fuss, to make him better, take his pain away. His rage and guilt were palpable, like some backpack he carried around with him day and night. He was only human, she wanted to tell him, and that we all made some bad choices sometimes. That we lived with the consequences and did the best we could. That guilt wasn't useful; it couldn't be turned into positive energy, that it just rotted away from the inside and destroyed its host.

Blah blah blah, she thought. Fine sentiments, worthy of a radio shrink.

All he needed from her was to let him be alone with his grief.

The whistling of the kettle interrupted her thoughts and she returned to the kitchen for her tea.

In truth, how *could* she understand the magnitude of what he'd been through? Except for the death of her beloved father—too soon, but still the natural order of things—she really hadn't experienced much more heartbreak than adolescent breakups and the death of a pet.

This was the death, not only of a once-loved spouse, but of a child. God, it was *wrong*, out of order. Unacceptable. And she could hurt with him but she couldn't hurt for him. Although if she could take some of it from him, she would do so, gladly.

Shannon heard the balcony door sliding open, then shut. She left her tea brewing on the counter, came out to face him. His expression was cold and hard, his jaw set like steel.

"I'm going to get them. I'm going to get those sons of bitches."

"Good." There was not only cold determination on his face, but in his eyes she saw something more, something wild and uncivilized. It made her shiver. "Mitch?"

"What?" he snapped. "I don't need any lectures on how revenge is bad for the soul."

"You won't hear them from me. I'm a complete believer in getting even, trust me. Right now, we're gathering data, witnesses, cases, all against Jonah-Dawn, and I hope you'll participate."

"What will that do?"

"It will close them down, for starters."

"So what?"

"So what? Think of all the innocent people they've duped, whose lives they've ruined."

"I'll leave you and others like you to think about that, to get justice for all of them. I'm thinking of more personal justice here." His voice as cold as a midwestern winter, he went on. "I intend to kill Jonah."

Hand over her heart, she hissed in a breath. "Mitch."

"And his wife, too. I intend to make them both suffer

the way I've been suffering, the way poor Joan and my little Jamie suffered."

"But—"

He cut her off with an emphatic shake of his head. "You go right ahead, Shannon. Put them out of business. Not enough for me. Not nearly enough. They go broke, so what? Does that bring my son back?"

"Does killing someone, anyone, bring him back? Will Jamie be here, with you, in the flesh, after you're done?"

His head snapped back as though he'd been hit. "God! Don't you ever know when to keep your mouth shut?"

"I'm trying to talk some sense into you here. You can't go around killing people."

"Sure you can. When you don't give a damn about the consequences. Oh, yeah, you sure can."

She opened her mouth to answer him but was stopped by his raised hand, palm out, warning her not to. "Enough," he said. "No more, Shannon. Enough."

With that, he stormed into the guest room and slammed the door.

Mitch paced, back and forth, back and forth, unable to contain his body's raging energy, until he couldn't stay on his feet anymore. Then he sank onto the edge of the bed and sat there, every muscle in his body quivering, his jaw so tight he wondered if he'd crush his teeth.

But he didn't care. He needed to *get* them, needed to buy a gun or build a bomb or drive a car through that huge, obscene bedroom of theirs while they were sleeping.

He needed to…

Help me, Daddy.

"Jamie, please," he said aloud. "Please, please, stop torturing me. I can't help you. Not then, not now."

He lay back on the bed, one arm slung over his eyes. He gave a brief thought to doing something to put himself out of his misery. What did they call suicide? A permanent solution to a temporary problem? But this wasn't temporary. His body hurt; his head ached; hell, his heart was in pieces. The pain wouldn't stop, not now, not ever.

Nor would the fierce rage deep in his gut, rage that had a life of its own. Rage at life, at death, but most of all, at himself. It was there, churning up inside him like a tornado.

He turned onto his side, pounded the bed with his good hand, again and again and again. There was no relief for him. No place he could go to escape. No place at all.

Chapter 7

Shannon sat for a long time, drinking her tea, staring at the fire while chastising herself. She'd pushed him too hard. Mitch had needed to vent and she should have let him. People always say they're going to kill people but they don't really mean it, she told herself, going for reassurance.

But what if he did mean it? She'd had more than just a glimpse of that primal rage in him. Beneath whatever veneer of civilization he'd developed in his journey from a hardscrabble childhood to the top of the business world there lay a man capable of giving in to the animal instinct to destroy an enemy.

But sometimes rage turned inward. Worried, she

eyed the door of the guest room. He'd told her to back off. But could she? Should she? When faced with a tough call, Shannon usually asked herself what was the worst thing that could happen. So she asked it now. The answer was: he would dump some more of his anger on her. Maybe lots more. Maybe even hate her.

But he wouldn't hurt her, physically, she was sure of it. Or pretty sure, anyway. Well, hey, she could take someone being pissed off at her; it had happened a lot in her career. Lawyers aroused antagonism naturally; it was what happened in the advocacy system— there was your side and theirs. If Mitch dumped a little rage on her, it wouldn't be pleasant, but she'd get over it.

And right now, *her* feelings were beside the point.

She walked to the door of the guest room, knocked softly, waited. No answer. She knocked again. "Mitch? Are you okay?"

"Go away, Shannon. Leave me alone."

"Only if you promise me you won't do anything stupid until you calm down."

"Promise you?" he asked, then followed that with a bitter chuckle. "Promise you," he repeated, more thoughtfully this time. "No. Sorry. Can't do it."

That took care of that.

There was no lock on the door, thank heaven, so she pushed it open partway and looked in. Her eyes widened; her mouth dropped open. He lay on the bed, his head propped up against a pillow, his arms flung out to the side. The clothing he'd been wearing was strewn all over the floor.

He was completely naked.

What she ought to do, she knew, was say, "Oops," give a cute little apology and close the door. But not Shannon. She was too busy looking.

Yes, Mitch was currently a bit too lean, and there were bruises, a few dressings, that bandage and splint on his left wrist and hand. But none of those were enough to take away from the fact that he possessed one mighty fine body. A warm, golden color. Long and lean, with sturdy, ropy musculature on his arms and legs, a sprinkling of silver and black hair on his chest, a nest of all-black hair surrounding his sexual equipment.

Which, when her gaze landed right there, gave a stir and began to thicken. It was almost as if it was saying hello to her. The thought, the ludicrousness of it, especially in the midst of serious concerns about life and death, caused a giggle to rise in the back of her throat. One inspired, of course, more by hysteria than amusement, but still… She clamped her hand over her mouth to stop the giggle in its tracks.

His eyes became slits. "What's so damned funny?"

Oh, no, he thought she was laughing at him. Unable to answer, she shook her head, too busy tamping down a rising hysteria to speak. Body shaking, bursting with the need to laugh out loud and relieve the tension, she held up a finger to signal he should give her a moment.

Instead of following her instructions, Mitch rose from the bed and came toward her. She followed his progress, her eyes widening, her fit of the giggles gone as quickly as it had come. He stood, towering over her, staring down at her. He was close enough for her to see the thin film of perspiration on his skin, to smell the earthy, thoroughly male odor of it, to observe the pulse in his neck throbbing at a breakneck speed.

"I said, what are you laughing at?"

His eyes, not filled with pain and heartache now, but with a curious mixture of cold anger and heat, drew her in, as they always did. His nostrils flared; his breathing rate increased.

She found herself uncharacteristically unable to utter a word.

He raised his right hand, clamped it on her upper arm. "Shannon," he said with a growl, shaking her. "I want you to leave this room right now."

At his touch, something shifted inside her, another mood swing, another dimension to the complex emotions swirling between them. A delicious sensation of warmth oozed through her bloodstream; a rising excitement stirred her every nerve ending.

"Or you'll do what?" It came out husky, a dare.

The muscles in his jaw throbbing as rapidly as his pulse, Mitch stared at her, for what seemed a long, long time. His grip on her arm was so tight it began to hurt. She shrugged out of his hold, making him look down at his hand as though it were a foreign object.

Then he met her gaze again. "Get out of here, Shannon. I mean it." With a muttered curse, he turned away from her, his fist clenched, and walked back toward the bed.

She watched the movement of his small, tight buttocks, the long thighs, the runner's wide calf muscles that tapered down to narrow ankles. Men had the best legs, she'd always thought. All elongated bone and muscle, none of that extra adipose tissue women had that covered and concealed their basic structure.

And Mitch's were a classic example of really, *really* nice male legs.

"And if I don't?" she challenged again.

He stood, kept his back to her. His every muscle was tense, on alert. Including, she was pretty sure, that very specific muscle between his legs. "Then I might not be responsible for what happens," he said darkly.

She leaned against the doorway, crossed her arms under her breasts. "We talking whips and chains? Or just some really intense one-on-one sex? Sorry, not up for the first, but I could *really* be talked into the second."

With a graphic curse, he whirled around, stared at her, his expression flashing perplexed amazement. "There goes that mouth again."

Okay, that did it.

Leaving the safety of the doorway, Shannon walked toward him, doing her best to appear sultry— not easy at less than five feet—but at least keeping direct, challenging eye contact with him. When she was standing only inches from him, she reached up a hand and ran her index finger down the middle of his chest. The hair was springy and thick; she wanted to run her cheek over it, let it tickle her face before she licked his nipples.

She raised her head and looked right into his magical eyes. "What was that about my mouth?"

She watched the change in his gaze as it morphed from bleak and angry to something equally intense but quite a bit hotter. Then, as though he'd given up, he said, "This," grabbed the back of her head with one hand, used his other arm to pull her up to him, so that her feet dangled off the ground, and attacked her mouth.

Not kissed. Attacked. From the start it was as if he was waging a war of conquer or die. Despite the previous wordplay, she was initially taken back by the savagery with which he plundered her mouth. He used tongue and teeth, pressing hard, taking quick nips, his breath hot, invading, not giving her a chance to catch her breath. She panicked momentarily, brought her hands up flat against his chest, pushed hard.

At once he released his hold on the back of her head, loosened the grip he had on the rest of her, and she found her feet back on the ground, locking eyes with a madman. "You get it now?" he growled.

No, not a madman, a mad man. A man with so much anger he had nowhere to put it. But a man who, when she pushed against him, had released her immediately. She had her answer now.

"I not only get it, I want it. Now."

With that, she pulled up her sweater, unhooked her bra and jeans, stripped off her socks, and within seconds was as naked as he was. Eyelids at half-mast, his gaze raked her body, his fist opening and closing, opening and closing at his side. She felt her nipples peaking under his gaze and the return of that same warm moisture between her thighs that she'd experienced last night in the kitchen. All this from one kiss. Good Lord, what would it be like when he actually touched her?

Condoms.

The thought whooshed into her head out of nowhere. Safe-sex training went deep. Darn, darn, darn. He wouldn't have any—he'd been homeless, for heaven's sake. She had some… Where? In her bedroom.

Just as Mitch reached for her, she backed away. It threw him momentarily. "Shannon?"

"Mitch?"

He took a step toward her, reached for her again. She backed away again, but she sent him an I-dare-you smile the whole time. He got into it then—not with a smile, but more determination. The man liked competition, and was used to coming out on top. On top was fine with her. On the bottom worked just as well.

This time he lunged at her, but she sidestepped him, turned her back, tossed a come-hither look over her shoulder, then said, "I need a larger bed than this one. You?"

She took off at a run for her bedroom; he was right

behind her, catching her from behind as she crossed the
threshold of her room. He wrapped his arms around her
waist and lifted her up against his chest, headed for the
bed. She laughed with pleasure. His right hand covered
one breast; she closed her eyes, threw her arms back and
clamped them behind his neck, then arched her back.
He sucked on her earlobe; she could feel his engorged
member poking at the top of her buttocks. They fell
onto the bed together, all legs and arms, mouths and
tongues, and tore into each other, like lovers who had
been apart too long and couldn't wait for nighttime.

Somewhere in the swirl of sensation, she gave a
brief thought to his wounds, to the bandage on his left
hand. But he seemed to be handling himself just fine
and she made the instant decision not to worry about
that. He was a grown-up, he'd told her, and oh, yes, oh,
oh, oh, yes! he most definitely was.

Mitch could barely contain himself. He felt frantic
with desire, nearly out of control, but anything he
dished out, Shannon took with astonishing eagerness.
He needed to taste her, all of her, and not gently either.
It seemed fine with her; she held back nothing, gave as
good as she got. Her small, sturdy body turned him on
nearly beyond endurance. Neither of them stopped
moving; neither of them seemed able to. He was dimly
aware through the haze of raw sensuality filling his
brain that his anger had turned into sexual frenzy, just
as intense, just as deep, but with a promise of pleasur-
able release instead of more rage.

He raked her skin with his teeth; she raked his back with her nails. He licked her and bit her, all over, tasting the skin he'd longed to touch for days, sucking on it, sucking on her nipples, her neck, the backs of her knees, and the hard bud in the folds of her vagina.

It was as if neither of them could decide on a position, so they tried them all. He brought her to climax with his mouth, and the minute her spasms slowed down, he did it all over again. Before he could take her over the top a third time, she bucked, moved her small body around, and took him in her mouth. There was nothing delicate about the way she lavished it with her tongue, nothing subtle about the way she drew him in and sucked on him.

It was pure agony; it was glorious. He wanted to die, not from pain but from pleasure. She did something with the back of her throat and took in all of him, up to the hilt, and that was when he knew he wasn't going to make it anymore.

He withdrew from her, took both her hands in his right one, cursed the fact that he had very little use of his left, and growled, "I want in. Now."

Her breath was coming so fast, Mitch wondered if she felt as light-headed as he did. "Drawer in table," she managed to say.

He couldn't reach over with his bandaged hand, so he said, "Stay right where you are."

Amazingly enough she did, kept her hands over her head, her wrists crossed, as though he'd tied them there.

He pulled open the drawer, found several packages of condoms, took out a few—always be prepared—then ripped one open with his mouth and rolled it on. It probably took ten seconds, and the minute he was done, he grabbed her hands again, brought his left arm under her, tipped her hips up and plunged in. He relished the way she cried out, not in pain, but in welcome.

Even here they warred with each other. He could see from her eyes that she was dazed with erotic passion, but instead of closing them and giving herself over, she kept them open, trained on him, daring him to push her even further.

He used the only weapon he had and did just as she asked. He pulled partway out and plunged again, reared back and plunged again. Every time he did, her eyes widened with surprise. He loved that look, loved that he could master her this way, in the age-old way that men had been mastering women since time immemorial.

"I want you to come," he whispered, plunging in again and again.

"Do you?" She thrust her hips up, tightened her inner muscles, created absolute agony for him.

And still he kept on. "Yeah."

"Well, all I can say is…Oh!" Her eyelids fluttered. "Oh, Mitch!"

Her hips moved faster and faster; he moved faster and faster with her. He was on the verge, but he gritted his teeth. "Do it, Shannon. Damn you, do it!"

She did. A sound began low and deep in the back of

her throat, then burst forward into an all-out scream. Eyes closed, her head jerked from side to side as she arched her back and clamped down on him, her inner muscles spasming.

Then, and only then, would he let himself go. With his own cry of completion, his body pumped everything he had into her, all the rage, all the frustration, all the built-up tension he'd been carrying around, it felt, for years. When he was done, he collapsed onto her, then rolled off, just in case he was too heavy for her.

They lay side by side for a long, long time, not speaking. He moved his right arm under her neck—she was so small, how the hell had she gotten through all that?—and pulled her close. Within moments, he was sound asleep.

For quite a long time, Shannon's mind was blank. This was not the normal state of her mind, and she kind of enjoyed it. Eventually, when her heart rate had returned to normal, and she could hear Mitch's deep, even breathing next to her, and she knew he was asleep, she considered what had just happened.

She felt… What was the right word? Conquered. Vanquished. She'd fought the good fight but the enemy had won. No, no, not the enemy, not even close; primitive caveman had clubbed primitive cave woman and carried her off to his cave then had his way with her? Closer. Only they'd both carried each other off. And it hadn't been against her will, oh no, far from it. She'd reveled in it. That sense of being, what? Tamed? Not quite the right word either. Put in her place? Please.

No, it was *conquered*, that was the word, and that was all there was to it.

Wow, what was that about?

Sex had never been like this. Just the opposite. She'd latched onto men who were at a down time in their lives. They'd been needy; she'd been in control. She'd picked them; they'd responded; she'd brought them warmth and healing and good sex so they could get back on their feet and thrive.

Elsewhere.

Always elsewhere. That was how she'd wanted it. Fix them and send them on their way, let her get back to her mission in life, her work.

Not this time. What had just happened between her and Mitch had not an element of healing or warmth to it. And if she'd provoked him at the beginning, by the end she'd certainly had no control. None. He'd had it all. Her body felt used, weak. Conquered.

And utterly satisfied.

Hey, she thought in the moment before slipping into sleep, not a bad way to feel. No sir, not a bad way at all.

Once in a while.

Mitch thought long and hard about a lot of things the next morning, but he waited until he heard Shannon leave for work before opening his eyes. Then he threw on his sweats, poured himself a cup of the coffee she'd so generously left for him, and headed for the phone in the living room. Now that he knew it was nothing in his New Hampshire life that had prompted the attack on him, he had to face up to his responsibilities.

He called his office, asking for Mel, his second in command. When the other man had gotten past the initial shock of hearing from him, very much alive, Mitch filled him in briefly on recent events and told him he was on the mend, but asked Mel not to let the media know, not yet; he wasn't ready to face public scrutiny. And then, finally, he asked how the business was doing.

"Not real well, needless to say."

Mitch heard the sarcasm and the underlying hurt and anger from his second in command, and he couldn't blame him, not in the least.

"The entire Brussels deal fell through after you disappeared. I've been juggling all kinds of balls in the air until I got word, one way or another. I'm really glad you're okay, Mitch," he said quickly, but the sense of betrayal leaked through, "but we need you back here right away. Yesterday. If you want to salvage anything, that is. If you don't, then hey, I guess a hell of a lot of people will be out of work."

A stab of self-recrimination hit Mitch right in the solar plexus. In his grief, he'd again acted in his own best interests, not thinking of how his actions would affect others. How much more guilt, he wondered idly, could he withstand before imploding?

"I won't let that happen, Mel. I promise. I'm sorry, that's all I can say."

"Yeah, well, you know what they say sorry will get you."

"Look, I'll call you later today. We'll get it all worked out. Trust me."

The silence on the other end of the line let him know just how well that one had gone over.

As he disconnected he wondered why he hadn't told Mel he'd be on the first flight out of there. Was it because he didn't want to leave all the unanswered questions he had about Joan and Jamie's last days?

No, the real reason he was putting off leaving could be summed up in one word: *Shannon.*

What was his responsibility to her now? Especially after last night's— What had she called it? Really intense one-on-one sex? He allowed himself a brief smile at the memory of her standing before him, the top of her head not even reaching his shoulders, her brown eyes issuing a challenge, which he'd been only too glad to take up.

He sighed, raked his fingers through his hair. The whole thing had been thoroughly, totally exhilarating. And bordering on scary. Sex born of rage, just at the edge of madness. Most women would have turned tail and headed for the hills. But then, she wasn't most women, was she?

He found her card and punched in the numbers.

"Shannon Coyle," he heard her say.

"Hi," he said.

"Hi yourself," she said back, then "Hold on." She directed the next part to someone else. "I'll be just a minute, Mac." Then, after another few moments, she said, "Okay, we're alone now. How are you doing?"

"I was about to ask you the same thing. Are you okay? It got a little rough last night."

"More to the point, how are you? You were convalescing, if I remember correctly."

"I'm fine, really I am. But seriously, are you okay?"

"I am somewhat sore in places I didn't know existed," she said with a smile in her voice, "but nah, I'm all right. I'm short but I'm sturdy."

Did this woman take cheerful injections each morning? Their natures were so directly opposite—Mitch's was dark; he woke up prepared for trouble and bad news and fought his way out of that all day. It had been like that even before the recent tragedies.

"Even so," he told her, "I wanted to apologize."

"For what?"

"Taking out my black mood on you. I crossed a line."

"Nope, sorry. I won't accept that. I was willing."

God, she could be frustrating. "Look, Shannon, you might have been willing but I'm a hell of a lot bigger and stronger than you are and once we got started, if you'd wanted me to stop I probably wouldn't have been able to."

"I don't recall asking you to stop."

"Damn. You're just not going to let me do this, are you?"

"What? Add one more person to your guilt list? Sew a button on your hair shirt? Sorry, not interested in being a member of the club."

Impossible. The woman was impossible.

"Whatever," he said with a weary sigh. "Okay, look. I called my office."

That seemed to shut down the conversation midstream. When she did speak, he could sense a change. "Oh? How did that go?"

"The business is floundering, which doesn't surprise me, so I have to get back there ASAP, put in an appearance, shore up the troops."

"Of course."

"But, I, uh, want you to know that you saved my life and I can't express enough thanks for that."

"You know what? Take your thanks and shove it." With that, she hung up.

Puzzled, he stared at the phone. What the hell had he said? He was debating whether or not to call her back when the phone rang.

"Sorry," Shannon said. "Not your fault. You hit a button there."

"What kind of button?"

"Some other time," she said breezily, and he knew he'd get no answer right then. "So, when are you leaving?"

"Probably tomorrow. But I want to discuss that suit you're talking about at some length. The one against JonahDawn. I'll front all expenses. You have a blank check."

"Not a smart thing to say to a not-for-profit, you know."

"I trust you."

"Uh-oh."

Mitch had to smile. "You got a problem with me trusting you?"

Her response wasn't immediate, but when she did reply, all traces of her usual flippancy were absent. "No. I'm flattered. Thanks. And on behalf of the others to be named in whoever, et al versus JonahDawn, I thank you also."

"And I'm moving into a hotel today." He'd just made up his mind to do that. Whatever she said to the contrary, he wasn't going to allow a repeat of what had happened last night. Not until, and if, he was a little more settled inside.

"Oh?" A brief pause. Then she said, "I'll miss you. I kind of liked having a roommate."

"I kind of liked being your roommate."

The silence that followed was different, more subtle, redolent of warm, morning-after sheets and blankets.

"I'd like to take you out to dinner tonight," he said. "We can discuss the case." He chuckled. "I'll have access to my credit cards again."

She didn't answer right away, and he could swear he heard her brain clicking away. "Well, sure. That would be nice."

"I'll call you later with details."

"I look forward to it."

He sat for a moment after they'd hung up and stared at the phone. She hadn't sounded more than mildly pleased to be asked out, and he realized he'd gotten used to that musical lilt in her voice, the one that reminded him of spring and hope and good cheer. The one that seduced him, made him think momentarily of life instead of death.

Good, then. He didn't want her to be pleased to be with him. It was too tempting; he couldn't afford that.

He had a purpose now. He'd decided not to go after the Dentons himself. An amateur, he might botch it. There was a quote he'd been thinking about that morning: "Revenge is a dish best served cold," or something to that effect. He would wait. First they'd do it legally; he'd front the money to hire top investigators, gather proof that they'd had a hand in Joan and Jamie's deaths, present it all to the authorities. If there was a trial, and they were found guilty and were sent off to jail for life, fine.

If it didn't get to trial, or it did and they were cleared, then he knew what he had to do. He didn't have to be in a hurry, didn't have to act impetuously. He had patience and resources.

But one thing he did know. The founders of Jonah-Dawn had to pay.

When Shannon hung up from Mitch, she wasn't sure just how she was supposed to feel. Not like this, though. Not confused and unhappy and rudderless, with this sense of something left unsaid, unfinished. She'd craved a little morning-after sweet talk; instead she'd gotten an apology. An apology! For what? Maybe the most exciting night of her life? Excuse me?

Why had the conversation gone the way it had? What had she done wrong? Had she expressed too much need for him last night? Been too voracious? Had that turned him off? Well, not entirely. She comforted herself with the fact that he'd invited her to dinner. To discuss the case. Ugh. Not exactly the way she'd have written the scene.

She chewed on her thumbnail, frowning, her insides in a knot. She'd never really done this before, fretted about what a guy was thinking about her. Other girls had gotten into that, worried themselves sick about if he'd call, if he'd call again, if he cared, if she was enough or too much for him. Never Shannon, or rarely, anyway; sure she'd had the usual human amount of self-doubt, but it had never lasted very long. She'd been above all that "female" stuff. Too busy righting wrongs and saving society.

Until Mitch had come into her life—was it just a week ago?—and thrown her for a loop. It was payback time now for all those teenage and early twenties conversations with friends when she'd sat there and told them to shape up, get a spine, have a little pride. Oh, boy, it was sure payback now.

She hated it.

But she'd have to get past it because she had a job to do.

She went out to the main room. No clients at the moment. Mac was at his desk, making notes.

"So," she said, stopping by Lupe's desk to grab a lemon bar before heading for Mac's. "You're sure about that call from Callie? She's all right? Shaved her head and we're not to worry?"

"Yup."

"Don't worry. Right." She plopped herself onto his visitor's chair. "Anyhow, I got some more lowdown on JonahDawn. Apparently the compound is run modestly, but the master bedroom looks like a bordello."

When she finished with details, Mac shook his head. "Something wrong with that picture."

"Yeah."

"Where'd you get this?"

"From Mitch."

"Mitch?"

"Mitchell Connor," she said with a breezy wave of her hand, "our formerly homeless beating victim now revealed to be a captain of industry."

"How's he doing?"

"Pretty well, actually." She glanced down at her thumbnail. It was ragged, needed some filing. And one of these days she was going to find time for a manicure.

"You talked to him over the weekend?"

"You could say that." She studied her other hand. "He's, uh, been staying with me."

"Excuse me?"

She made herself look up, meet his gaze. "Don't, Mac."

"Don't what?"

"I don't know. Whatever you were going to say, don't."

His dark brown eyes, paler with age and set deep in surrounding mocha-colored wrinkles, closed once. Then he shook his head and opened them again. "Now I got both Callie and you to fret over," he said indignantly. "And I don't like to fret. Thought I gave it up when I left the force. Thought I'd go fishing, get a hobby, take up golf. But no, I had to come onboard here, help to save mankind."

"You love it here and you know it."

"*Love* is too strong a word. But I'm sure not bored, that much I'll tell you, not with all these young women running off and doing stupid things."

"I resent that. I'm a grown woman who makes choices and I live with them." She grinned. "Anyway, we have a blank check from my…houseguest to get started on our JonahDawn attack."

"Do tell." That cheered him up.

"Maybe we can bat around a wrongful death suit."

"In which case I'm going to contact some old buddies, get a copy of the accident report, see how thorough the investigation was."

"Terrific."

She rose just as the front doorbell jingled and a white-haired, stooped woman using a walker was ushered into the reception area by a young, pimply faced teenager with an iPod in one ear and a cell phone in the other. Lupe stood to greet them; Shannon headed for her office.

"I'm going to make some calls, too," she said to Mac over her shoulder. "Get this thing rolling."

Chapter 8

He was staying at one of the top Santa Monica hotels, and its restaurant was also highly rated, so Shannon decided to go all out. She found the time to get a manicure and a pedicure. She wore soft, pretty clothing, a coral V-neck sweater, one that actually showed whatever cleavage she could muster, a flower-patterned skirt that swished back and forth as she walked, two-inch sandals. A thin gold chain around her neck and gold drop earrings made her feel elegant, and she pulled her curls off her face with a pair of tiny coral combs. She even took care with her makeup—eyeliner, shadow and mascara, blush. Lipstick that matched her sweater. Otherwise known as the Works. If Mitchell Connor thought he was going to forget her, she had some news for him.

However, when she hurried into the restaurant ten minutes late, it was his appearance that made her mouth drop open. He stood in profile near the reception desk, and she halted in her tracks and stared. Ohmygod, he was gorgeous. He had real clothing on—a dark gray turtleneck sweater and perfectly fitted black pants were exactly right for his coloring. She made herself move toward him, and as she did, she saw that he'd had his hair cut.

The wrist bandage and splint were gone; his cheekbones were prominent, his jawline immaculate, and she thought she might faint from the beauty of the man.

She came up behind him and tapped him on the shoulder. "Not bad for a street person."

He turned around and grinned at her. Actually grinned. Her heart went pitty-pat at the sight of all those lovely white teeth.

His gaze was appreciative. "You look pretty good yourself."

"What's up with your wrist?" Shannon asked, swallowing down the urge to slather him with kisses.

"I went to an orthopedic doctor today. He said the sprain is coming along and gave me a removable splint."

"You also went to a clothing store and a barber and a hairstylist."

He raised his hand and stroked his clean chin. "Amazing what you can do with a credit card. Come."

As they were shown to an ocean-view table,

Shannon was struck not only by the ease with which he handled himself—the man was used to first-class treatment, no doubt about it—but by the dichotomy of Mitch in his designer clothing tonight and Mitch in his homeless rags last week. An amazing difference; clothes, not to mention hair, both the facial and the head-covering kind, really did make the man.

The table was candlelit, the crystal perfect. The soft murmur of other diners accompanied the muted sound of ocean waves that managed to be heard through thick glass windows. The setting was elegant and very romantic.

Only the minute they sat down and ordered cocktails, Mitch asked her to bring him up to date on the entire JonahDawn case, start to finish. He wanted to know all about Callie and Mac, and everything they knew so far about the Dentons. He peppered her with questions; Shannon answered. Somewhere in there they ordered, she ate two or three heavenly sourdough rolls with butter, drank a martini and said no to a second, and their meals were served. It was much more of a working business dinner instead of what she'd fantasized, which was a chance for Mitch and her to get to know each other, to start over, to see and appreciate each other. Or, rather, *he* was to see and appreciate that she was, apart from a lawyer and caregiver, an actual flesh-and-blood woman.

But except for his initial greeting, which had been warmly approving, his attitude had been thoroughly impersonal. Not to mention intense, somewhat abrupt and dictatorial. She was starting to chafe under the onslaught.

"I want you to hire more investigators if you need to," he told her when their plates had been cleared.

"I'm planning to. I'm hoping Callie will be back in a couple of days or else I'll have to look for part-time legal help."

"You have other clients, don't you?"

"Lots of them."

"Hire as much help as you need. I want you to devote all your attention to JonahDawn."

"You 'want' me to? Hold on." Okay, now she was becoming truly irritated. "You're barking orders at me like I'm some peasant and you're the king of the world."

He seemed taken aback, as though he had no idea what she was talking about.

"I don't work for you, Mitch."

He raised an eyebrow. "Oh? I thought you were my lawyer."

"Correct. Your lawyer, not your servant. But you're not my sole client, and I'm not going after JonahDawn because you'd like some closure. I'm going after them for you *and* for what looks like a whole slew of others who've been victimized by them."

"Thanks. I feel really special now."

"What is it, Mitch? Why am I sensing so much urgency? And distance, too? Why can't we relax a little, enjoy being together?"

Mitch knew she was right, but he didn't know how

to reply, so he kept quiet, signaled the waiter and ordered an after-dinner brandy.

She cocked her head to one side, studied him with eyes that saw way too deeply into his insides. "Or is this your basic personality and I wasn't privy to it before now?"

"Joan used to tell me I had two moods," he admitted. "Black and dark gray."

"Well now, isn't that a pleasant way to live your life."

"Not particularly. But that's how she saw me, and I guess, when we were together, especially those last few years, it was true." He shook his head. "See? I'm doing it again. Telling you my darkest secrets."

She reached over, placed her hand on top of his, squeezed. "I'm glad you are."

He hesitated before saying, "Are you sure it was okay last night?"

"Mitchell Connor," she said, obviously exasperated with him, "it was just about the best sex I ever had. Which means it was more than okay. It was…superlative."

"Really?" He knew his sudden smile was the pleased, smug, male kind but that was how he felt. "Really?" he said again.

"You want me to fill out a scorecard? Foreplay, technique, intensity, durability, fit, postcoital snuggling. All a definite ten."

He sat back in his chair, thrown, and not really sure why.

"You seem surprised."

He considered for a moment, then told her the truth. "You know, I am. In my youth, I was considered…a pretty decent bed partner. But then—" He stopped himself. "No. I'm not going to go there."

"Not going to talk about your sex life with Joan? Hey, in a troubled marriage, that's where it usually shows up." He was about to protest, out of some old-fashioned sense of chivalry, but she held up her hand. "Not my business. Really. I just want you to know that whatever kind of a lover you were, as you say, in your youth, you're back. And probably even better. Older and smarter and just plain yummy."

That got a chuckle out of him.

The waiter served his brandy then, and Mitch deduced from the smirk on his face that he'd likely heard at least the last part of their conversation. He waited for the man to leave, then studied Shannon's face, the bouncy curls, the bright brown eyes. "What is it about you?"

"What?"

"You say pretty much whatever's in your head, things most people wouldn't dare say out loud, and you get away with it."

"A couple of judges and a lot of prosecutors would not agree."

"You know what I mean. You're probably the first one hundred–percent honest woman, hell, honest *anyone*, I've ever met."

This time she held up both hands in protest. "Hey, don't make me out to be a saint. Far from it. I can be devious if called for. I can lie. Although most of the time I don't because, frankly, I don't do it very well. But I can lie to myself, big time. Sweep stuff under the rug that I don't want to look at. Believe me."

"Like what?"

Like the fact that I'm sitting here across the table from you and I just realized I'm in love with you.

That was the way it came to Shannon, out of nowhere, fast and furious like an on-target missile. It landed in her brain with total certainty, and it took all the effort she could muster not to verbalize it. Despite her suddenly rapidly beating heart, she went for a casual shrug, picked up her butter knife, spread some on another roll. "You know. Everyday things."

"Like what?"

She scurried around in her head for examples, the kind she could say out loud. "Like I wondered if you thought my thighs were too large last night or my breasts too small. I don't take enough time for girl-type self care. If I could come back as anything, it would be as a six-foot blond model with straight hair and legs a mile long. What else. Sometimes I don't like my clients, want to shake them and say 'Stop with the self-pity, grow up, take some responsibility,' and then I hate myself afterwards because most of them truly never had a chance. You know, stuff like that."

"Are you afraid of anything?"

"What is this, an interview?"

"Are you?"

"Sure. Heights. Small airplanes. Being killed by a terrorist. Earthquakes. Big bad men in dark alleys. Going up against a really top lawyer in court and looking like I don't know what I'm doing. Growing old alone."

Uh-oh. That one shouldn't have slipped out. It was way too naked.

And Mitchell Connor, no fool he, picked right up on it. "So. You don't want to grow old alone."

"Not particularly." She smiled. "One day I'll get me a couple of cats, that should take care of it."

He sipped his brandy, studied her for a bit longer, and she began to grow uncomfortable under his scrutiny. "What?"

Mitch finally saw it, the quality he'd been wondering if she possessed, which, of course, she did. Just like every other human being on the planet, including him, Shannon had those soft, uncertain places inside her. She had needs. She wouldn't be quick to admit them, but they were there. She might actually occasionally need someone to lean on, to depend on, to take care of her.

Something deep within him shifted just slightly, causing a sense of calm to come over him that wasn't customary. He took her hand in his. "Hey."

She studied their joined hands. "Hey what?"

"Have I told you that you look beautiful tonight?"

"Nonsense." She looked down, played with her roll.

"Not nonsense. If I say it, it's so. And have I told you that I can't stand women with thin thighs and huge breasts?"

"Really?"

"Absolutely," he said solemnly, which made her cock her head to one side in that adorable way she had.

"How do you feel about really, really short women?"

"I'm learning to appreciate them."

"Well, now, isn't that nice?"

He spread her hand, palm up, on the table and used his thumb to trace the delicate blue veins of her wrist. "I came here tonight to say goodbye," he told her.

Her face fell. "Yeah, I figured."

"And I will have to say goodbye, tomorrow. I don't have a choice."

"I know."

"But it's still tonight, and I wonder if you'd like to come up to my hotel room." He lowered his voice to a seductive whisper. "It has the softest pillows I've ever experienced. And a huge bathtub with jets."

"Does it have a mirrored ceiling?"

"Sadly, no."

"Then I guess it's not perfect."

"Willing to settle for just this side of perfect?"

She considered, a frown forming between her perfect brows. "Should I play hard to get?"

"Why would you want to do that?"

"I don't know. They say it increases anticipation."

He brought her hand up to his mouth and gently

sucked on one of her fingers. "If you were to reach under the table and place your hand at the bottom of my zipper, you would have, shall we say, ample proof that I am already fully anticipating."

As his tongue laved the next finger, she shuddered. "And if you were to reach under the table and place your hand under my skirt and between my thighs—I'm wearing a see-through lace thong by the way—I believe you'd experience the same."

"Shall we?"

"Place our hands under the table?" she asked, her grin mischievous.

"What I want to do to you, I'd rather do in private." He leaned over and whispered in her ear, describing just what that was, in detail.

She gasped, said a soft "Oh," then stood. Her face was flushed and smooth in the candlelight. "Then I say we go for it."

It was different this time. One hundred–percent different. It was slow; it was tender. Mitch took the lead and she let him, wanted him to. She felt soft, all over.

He undressed her, taking his time, approving of her various body parts, showing that approval by stroking her, bestowing soft, sensual kisses all over, caressing her breasts, her thighs, murmuring that they were just right.

He had her sit in a chair, brought her knees over his shoulders, made love to her stomach, her inner thighs, the slick folds of her womanhood. Then they moved to the bed and he had her lie on her stomach; he ran his fingers up and down the backs of her legs, her ankles, sucking on her toes, tonguing the spaces between them. She discovered she had erogenous zones she never knew existed.

She was in a dream. Someone had granted a wish she didn't remember making to have a gorgeous man treat her as though she were the most desirable woman in the world. She floated on the newly discovered cloud of love she felt for him, took all his attentions and ministrations as his own declarations of love, even if that wasn't the truth. In the dream, it was.

At some point it became her turn to cherish him; first they filled the lavish tub with bath salts and soaked in it, then she made love to him. She couldn't seem to get enough of his body, all the fine hard planes of it, the subtle curve of his biceps, the strong line of his back. And those legs of his! She rubbed her cheek over the fine, springy body hair, sniffing the bath salts on him and amazed how they didn't smell feminine but only musky.

They loved each other, one at a time and together. It was a night to remember forever, to keep in her memory bank and take out on a cold winter night.

He couldn't be saying goodbye. She told herself that, surely, they'd find a way to see each other. If nothing else, this connection they had in bed, this *rightness,* well, who in his right mind would abandon this? Not possible.

At some point they could give each other nothing more. Exhausted and thoroughly sated, they slipped into sleep.

When Shannon awoke, it was still pretty early. Nearly six, according to the clock next to the extremely large bed, the one with lovely feather pillows and a thick duvet covered in a material as soft as any baby skin she'd ever stroked. She lay on her side, Mitch behind her, spoon fashion. One of his arms was draped over her waist, his hand cupping her breast. Could this be, she wondered sleepily, the definition of heaven on earth? She emitted a loud, contented sigh.

"You awake?" he murmured in her ear.

"Mmm."

He drew his arm back and changed positions; immediately, she missed his warmth. She turned over to see his head propped up against pillows, his arms folded behind his head.

She lay on her other side now, elbow bent, her head resting in her outstretched hand. The frown on his face was not to her liking.

"What?" she asked.

He gazed at her, those pale gray eyes of his silvery in the early morning light. "I wish we weren't so good together. I wish we'd met at a different time."

"Oh?"

He nodded, thoughtful. "You are an amazing woman, being with you is like—" he shrugged, as though searching for the words "—like a glimpse into a world I never knew existed. But I have nothing to give you, Shannon. I wish I did."

She did not like the tenor of this conversation. She scrambled up to a sitting position. "What brought all this up?"

"I didn't intend for it to get this far. I really was going to say goodbye to you last night. That's why I tried to focus on JonahDawn, why I tried to keep my distance. I didn't want you—" he blew out a breath "—to care for me, to expect anything from me."

She stifled her instant urge to say something cutting and defensive about his ego, about all male egos, because, of course, she did care for him. Heck, she'd fallen in love with him, which, even though she kept it to herself, he must have picked up on. Had she transmitted that message to him without words, and had that pushed him away? She felt exposed and uncomfortable.

She took some time to choose her response. "I do care about you, Mitch. And I think you care about me," she added, mostly believing it. "It's been a good thing. We came into each other's lives at the right time, that's all. You needed a friend and I was willing. I hadn't been intimate with a man for a long time and you were willing. We gave to each other, and I'm glad we did." She paused, swallowed. "But I get you. It's not going to happen. That makes me sad, but I'm a realist." She raised her head, gave what she hoped passed as a jaunty toss of curls. "And besides, it has to stop now anyway. I don't make a practice of sleeping with clients."

"What do you call what we did last night?"

"Not sleeping, for sure. Just a catnap or two."

She grinned, trying to invite him into her lighthearted-ness, but he was still in serious mode. "I mean it, Shannon. I wish we'd met, I don't know, in a year from now. You're such a special person."

Just what every woman wanted to hear. *You're such a special person.* One of those I-don't-love-you-but-I-wish-I-could phrases. Ugh.

She went for an easy shrug. "Hey, wishes don't make anything so. It is what it is. I'm a big girl. And I understand you're still grieving. I understand you have to leave and take care of your business and your life on the East Coast. It's okay." She caught herself before she piled it on too thick. "No, you say you value my honesty. Then let me be honest. I will miss you. A lot. But I'll get over it."

He studied her some more, then nodded and said gravely, "I hope I will."

Excellent answer, Mitch, she thought. Just excellent. One that left her with her pride intact. And gave her permission to say lightly "Call me, okay?"

"Well, if nothing else I'll need progress reports on the case."

"We'll do most of that by e-mail. You're going to be very busy saving your business."

"If it can be done," he said ruefully.

"You'll do it."

"Where did you get all this confidence in me?"

She cocked her head to one side, studied him. "You know, I'm not sure. I guess I have a gut feeling that you're a hard worker and pretty determined and won't give up until you absolutely have to."

One side of his beautiful mouth curved upward. "Sounds like a description of an extremely short, ridiculously energetic lady lawyer of my acquaintance."

"Does it? Hmm. What a formidable pair we are."

He didn't reply, because of course there still was no "we." They weren't a pair. And he had just told her they weren't going to be. For now. And she rarely allowed herself to engage in "maybe one day…" fantasies.

Totally unexpected and unwelcome tears began to gather at the back of her throat and behind her eyes. She would not let him see her cry over him. No way. She glanced at the clock again, then at her clothing scattered all over the thick carpet. "Oops." She scrambled out of bed. "I have to get moving. Got lots of dragons to slay today."

"You don't have time to stay a while? I thought I'd order room service."

"Nope," she said cheerfully. "Early court appearance."

"I'll walk you down."

"No need."

"But I will anyway."

As they dressed, she darted around in her head for something distracting to stave off the crying jag she knew she was about to have. She could worry some more about Callie, she supposed. There was Jonah

Denton's smug smile. Judge McLaughlin and his bad dentures that clicked when he talked.

By the time they were in the elevator, Shannon was pretty sure she'd avoided heading for an emotional meltdown. They stood side by side and silent on the way down, as though there'd been an unspoken agreement between them not to touch, not to remember what they'd shared the night before.

When the elevator doors opened, they walked along the corridor and into the hotel lobby. She was totally unprepared for the flashbulbs, the reporters crowding in on Mitch, darting questions back and forth.

"Mr. Connor, where have you been all this time?"

"Mitchell Connor! Did you have a nervous breakdown?"

"Mitch! Did you consider killing yourself?"

"Are you under doctor's care?"

"Will you declare bankruptcy?"

She held her arms out, palms facing the horde, ready to do battle for him, but Mitch's whisper was urgent. "Go. I'll handle it."

"But I'm your lawyer."

"Go," he said. "I want to keep you out of this."

She didn't want to go. She wanted to protect him, to defend him from the nosiness and the rudeness and the headline-hungry crowd of vultures. But he was right; she would be more effective in the background.

With a quick squeeze of her hand, Mitch pushed her away.

As she walked around the crowd and toward the front of the hotel, she heard one of the reporters say, "Who is that woman? Have you been staying with her?"

Mitch's reply, "We came down in the elevator together, that's all," stayed with her all the way to her car, where, after the door was closed and the key was in the ignition, she gave in to that crying jag after all.

The minute she got to the office, Mac rushed up to her. "Where the hell have you been?"

Taken aback, she said, "I'm sorry, I— What is it?"

"I got an SOS from Callie's phone an hour ago and I've been trying you all over the place."

She hadn't checked her voice mail while at home changing. Now she fumbled around in her purse, found her phone. Sure enough, she'd turned it off last night, hadn't wanted anything to interfere with her night with Mitch. That was twice this had happened while in his presence. Idiot, she cursed herself, as she turned it on again. There was a text message from Callie's phone, one that read SOS, and several from Mac after that.

Her heart thudded in her chest. "Okay. What do we do now?"

Mac pushed open the door she'd just closed behind her. "We get our asses up to the compound."

"Shouldn't we call the police?"

"Not officially, but Jackson's meeting us."

"Good move."

Detective Jackson Rutherford, Mac's former partner

and recently married to one of Shannon's good friends and occasional client, Vanessa Garner, was with the Pacific Community Police Department. He was also tall and very broad, without an ounce of fat on him, and spoke with a deceptively mild Southern accent. Jackson would present a formidable bit of "muscle" while accompanying one diminutive lawyer with a big mouth and one no-longer-in-top-shape retired police detective with more padding around his middle than was good for him.

That morning Shannon had told Mitch she had a court appearance, but that had been just an excuse for leaving quickly. In fact, her court calendar was clear, although she did have client appointments—an abused wife trying to leave her husband but afraid for her life, and a Jamaican cook whose boss kept docking his wages for minor infractions, leaving him with barely any paycheck at all. After leaving a note for Lupe to please reschedule her nine and ten o'clock meetings, Shannon followed Mac out the door.

They made it to Playa del Rey in about twelve minutes, where Jackson met them in front of the wrought-iron gate that led to the JonahDawn compound. He was in his detective gear—sports jacket, slacks and tie, but nothing could hide his massive chest and biceps.

"Hey, thanks, Jackson," she said, patting his rock-hard shoulder as she got into the back seat. Mac was in front, a steely expression on his face that she imagined he used to wear on the job, but that she hadn't seen much in evidence since he'd come to work at the Last House on the Block.

If she'd had to, she would have come up here alone, though no doubt about it, having the two men along felt not only safer but would present a much more imposing picture to the cult's leaders.

After they pushed the bell near the gate, and Jackson showed his ID to the camera, the gate swung open and they drove up the long driveway until they reached the castle. Built by some movie mogul with too much money and too little taste somewhere back in the 1920s, it was purported to be a replica of some Austrian prince's summer abode. Thick stonework, small high windows, at least four floors. Instead of crested flags waving from the top of the turrets, there were silk banners in sunshine colors, which relieved the basic gray-beige and white of the stonework and trim.

In front of the castle were about forty people of varying ages, all with shaved heads and wearing loose white clothing, working on flower beds and vegetable gardens on either side of the huge building. They looked up briefly at the car's arrival, then went back to hoeing and raking, weeding and watering. Shannon thought of monks at their toil.

The front door opened and they were ushered into a cavernous center hallway, lit by an enormous chandelier and surrounded by balconies. A pair of curved marble staircases, one at each end of the hall, led to the upper floors.

The woman who greeted them was about forty, dressed like all the others and sporting a pair of thick glasses. "Welcome," she said, although it didn't sound very welcoming. Not hostile, exactly, just lacking any kind of inflection whatever.

"Good morning, ma'am," Jackson said politely, flashing his badge. "We'd like to see Callie Kennedy, please."

"May I ask why?"

"We think she may be in some danger."

Her brow furrowed. "What kind of danger?"

"We'd like to talk to her. Please get her for us. We'll wait here."

"It's just that Father Jonah isn't here and—" She shook her head, seemed indecisive, as though waiting for instructions from an unseen power.

Shannon stepped around Jackson and planted herself. "Look, get her now or we'll have cops swarming all over this place, top to bottom, within the hour. Is that really what 'Father Jonah' would like?"

The woman's eyes widened behind her glasses, then she nodded. "I'll have someone fetch her right away," she said, hurrying off down a hallway.

Behind her, Shannon heard Jackson say, amused irony in his tone, "Now let's go over this one more time, Mac. You needed me here, why?"

She turned around in time to see Mac shrug. "A momentary lapse in judgment. Sorry."

"Hey, you guys," she protested, lightly punching Jackson on his arm. "You think I could have threatened her like that if I hadn't known you both were backing me up?"

Mac looked at Jackson, who returned his gaze, then together they both nodded. "Yeah," Jackson said, "seems to me you would have done the same thing with no one behind you while facing an entire battalion of armed cannibals."

"And one of these days," Mac said, less amused now, "it's going to get you in trouble."

"You're exaggerating, both of you."

At that moment, a bunch of bald, white-clad people came into the center hall from one of the numerous corridors leading off to the sides. Among them was, most definitely, Callie with a shorn head. The expression on her young face was more one of curiosity than anything else; she also didn't seem to be in any immediate danger that Shannon could see.

She raised a hand to her former intern, in a kind of weak greeting. "Hi, Callie."

"Hello, Shannon," she said calmly. "Mac."

When her gaze fell on Jackson, Shannon quickly said, "This is Jackson Rutherford, an old friend of Mac's."

Callie nodded to him, then shifted her attention back to Shannon, the expression on her face reminding her of the woman who had greeted them at the door. Neutral, almost disinterested. The group around her huddled close, as though protecting her.

Shannon wanted to pull her to her, hug her. But she didn't. "Are you all right?"

"Of course I am."

Mac said, "Callie, we got an SOS from you."

"A what?"

"On our cell phones. Both Shannon's and mine. It came from your cell phone. It said SOS."

"My cell phone?" She looked sideways at the others before saying calmly, "I don't have a cell phone. Or I did, but I threw it away the minute I got here. It's part of the Agreement." This last word obviously had some significance, as the others nodded, some murmuring, "The Agreement."

Shannon searched Callie's gaze, looking for a sign, a signal that she needed them to step in, that she was in some kind of danger but wasn't able to communicate it. "I'd like to talk to you alone."

"She doesn't need to talk to you alone." This came from a smallish man who seemed older than most of the others and whose voice was high-pitched and whiny.

The group murmured again, moved in even closer, reminding Shannon of a flock of very tall, very white penguins, forming a defense against a predator.

Jackson took hold of Shannon's arm and urged her aside. "Ms. Callie. Would you like to speak to Ms. Coyle alone?"

The young woman glanced quickly to her left and right, then back at Jackson, shaking her head. "No, I'm fine. I don't know why you're here."

"Because I'm worried about you," Shannon said.

"I told you I was quitting. I told you I was fine." Her

tone lost its calm. "I told you I don't want or need your help anymore."

Those around her spoke in soothing voices, saying, "Center, Sister Callie. Center."

Okay, Shannon thought, "Center" meant to chill out.

But she, for one, sure wasn't feeling very centered at the moment. Was Callie acting or had they actually gotten to her?

She placed her hands on her hips, feeling pugnacious. "Whatever all of you think, I'm of the belief that this entire setup is rotten and I—"

"Is there a problem?"

As one, they all turned to see Aurora as she glided in.

She was dressed in a long robe of vibrant colors and the contrast to the others was stunning. With her exotic Eastern features and gorgeous bone structure, not to mention her long, thick dark hair, she seemed to emit some kind of glow, a shimmering, otherworldly presence.

At her arrival, Callie's group backed off, not quite bowing but giving a pretty good imitation of awe in the presence of a deity.

"I am Sister Aurora," she announced calmly to the visitors. "May I be of help?"

Not *Mother*, but *Sister*, Shannon observed. Interesting hierarchy. Jonah was Big Daddy, all the others were his "children."

Jackson explained that they had reason to believe Callie was in some sort of danger and might need their aid. When he was done, Aurora turned to the group with a small serene smile. "Callie? You are in no danger here, but if you wish to leave, you may do so." All this was said with an eerie calm.

Callie replied fervently, "No. Please. Don't make me go back there."

More hysteria than necessary. An act? Had she been given drugs?

Aurora faced them again. "I think you heard her. Sister Callie is here of her own free will. And she wishes to stay."

Shannon addressed the assembled group. "Did any of you pick up a cell phone and punch in SOS?"

The murmurs of denial ceased when Aurora spoke again. "We don't have cell phones here. As soon as Sister Callie learned of our rule, she threw hers away."

"Where?"

"We recycle."

"And that means?"

"Exactly what it sounds like. Or aren't you familiar with the concept of doing what we can for our precious planet?"

Okay, Shannon thought, I didn't think I liked you before, now I know I don't like you. "I'd like to speak to your husband."

"Father Jonah isn't here at the moment."

"Oh? Where is he?"

That "gotcha" smile of serenity made Shannon want to wipe it off Aurora's face. "I don't believe that's any business of yours," she said calmly. "And now I'd like you to leave."

They really didn't have a choice. The two men turned to go, and after one last glance at Callie—who avoided meeting her eyes—Shannon followed them out.

As they were getting into Jackson's car, a figure appeared from the side of the castle. She recognized Louis Lee. He made brief eye contact with her, then looked away as another of JonahDawn's acolytes appeared in the doorway, as though making sure they were definitely leaving the property.

Fastening her seat belt, she wondered if Louis had been trying to contact her. Wishful thinking, most probably. It was more likely he was going to issue one of his not-very-veiled warnings about "being careful."

As the trio made their way back to Venice, Mac turned around and said, "Looks like we lost her, Shannon."

"I'm not one-hundred percent sure of that. What do you think Jackson?"

He met her gaze in the rearview mirror. "That is one weird bunch of folks. Back in Alabama we had some holy-roller types, a few Cajun witch doctors, a seer or two. I never felt much need for what they offered, but there are sure a lot of folks who are looking, that much I can tell you."

"Thanks, both of you," she said dryly. "If I was worried before, I'm even more worried now."

Chapter 9

From that moment on, Shannon rolled up her sleeves and got everyone at the Last House on the Block working their butts off. She not only hired two temp paralegals, she begged her usual volunteers—other lawyer friends who practiced a wide variety of legal disciplines, and who usually gave her a morning or afternoon one day a week—to give her more. They began the paperwork avalanche, issuing inquiry letters to JonahDawn's lawyers with the kinds of questions raised prior to potential lawsuits, hitting them with every issue the legal eagles could come up with. These had been suggested by Shannon's growing list of aggrieved clients and included the unusual amount of elderly people who had made the cult their conservators, the suspicion of exerting "undue influence" on the mentally incompetent, the possibility of forged documents.

They even found that the Playa del Rey compound was out of compliance with certain arcane property laws and threw that into the mix. Shannon and company fired darts all over the place; most wouldn't make it to the target but enough would. And in any event, Jonah and Aurora Denton were now on notice: the Last House on the Block was gunning for them.

If she gave an occasional thought to both Jonah and Louis's implied threats to her safety, she dismissed them, as she did most things that were fear-based. Shannon had long ago decided that if she dwelled on the things that scared her, it impeded forward momentum; that was intolerable to her.

Mac called in favors and got deep background on both the Dentons. Aurora turned out to have been arrested for running a sex-for-secrets ring, both political and economic, out of Singapore under the name of Padrah Bhandi, and trafficking in illegal substances out of Hong Kong under the name of Beng Gi. Both cases had been dismissed before coming to trial; rumor had it that not only had she had friends in high places, but the payoff amounts to let her remain free were enormous.

As for Jonah, he'd apparently led a quiet life in Cleveland as a married accountant with three children until six years before when, returning from a business trip to Washington, D.C., he'd sat next to a woman now known as Aurora Gee on the plane; three months later he'd left his family, his practice and the Midwest, and had headed out to the coast.

JonahDawn had begun slowly as a small religious sect with no name, meeting at a private home, and had taken its current name a year later. After which they'd purchased the compound in Playa del Rey and begun gathering more and more of a flock.

Shannon was itching to hire a forensic accountant to look into how they'd gotten the money for the castle, but there were too many details that were protected until and if she began legal proceedings. Mac called instead on one of his acquaintances, a surfer dude by the name of Benjamin D'Annunzio, whose computer skills were so amazing, he could find out pretty much everything about anything—unofficially, of course. Mac acted as intermediary between Ben and Shannon, who had no desire to be disbarred. However, if offered some third-party information, which was followed up using completely acceptable, legal means, well then, where was the problem?

One week went by, then two. And she was so busy she barely had time to think about Mitch…except late at night, lying awake in her suddenly lonely condo and her even lonelier bed, feeling an inner emptiness she didn't ever remember experiencing before. Maybe she shouldn't have made love with him before he'd left; the first time had been mostly intense, athletic sex. But that last time, no, that had been different. More of her core had been involved, deeply involved, as she'd brought the fact of her just-discovered love for him to bed with her. That last time had opened up too many possibilities for heartbreak and here it came. It hurt, pressed on her chest like an eighty-pound weight, which meant she woke up each morning not just tired and cranky, but with mild indigestion, too. Her appetite suffered.

She'd followed Mitch's fifteen minutes of fame in the news right after it had broken and was pleased there had been no mention at all of JonahDawn. Smart move on his part—they would take them by surprise. Through his attorney, he'd issued a statement to the press saying only that in his grief he had sought seclusion and that he would not be giving any details of where he'd spent his hiatus. He further requested that they respect his continued period of mourning for his late wife and child.

It was not enough, of course, for a voracious media, who for the next few days sent minions scurrying about the country looking for something sensational to uncover. But after Mitch's abandoned car was found and a couple of motel owners came forward to say he had spent the night at their establishments and that, no, there had been nothing of interest about his stay, it all died down, and the press went on to other more scandalous targets.

At some point, of course, especially if and when one of the nurses or orderlies who'd attended him in the hospital made the connection, it would start up again, but Shannon figured that future invasions of his private life, if necessary, would be dealt with then, in the future.

They corresponded about the case through e-mail, but she kept hoping he would call. As the days went on, she wondered why he *wasn't* calling. She thought about picking up the phone herself, asking how he was doing, was he feeling better, working too hard? But that old will-he-call-me-first *girl* thing came up every time she did. She didn't want to be her usual aggressive self, not this time, not with this man.

All of which pissed her off, because this entire bag of mental garbage meant she was letting her *personal* business interfere with her *business* business, something she truly tried to avoid. The whole thing sucked.

They heard no more from Callie, but Shannon called the compound every day and asked to speak to her, always being informed that Sister Callie was not available. She'd assumed she'd be told that, but she also figured her daily calls would let them know that someone was keeping tabs on the young woman, so any funny business would not go unnoticed.

Jackson was good enough to drive up there twice, flash his badge and insist on seeing for himself that Callie was still alive and well, which she was. But he didn't get to speak to her, just see her. And the second time, as he was leaving, he was informed that there would be no more visits from the police without a warrant, and that if he tried again, their lawyer was prepared to write up a harassment charge against Jackson.

When he called Shannon to report this latest development, he finished with "Looks like we're not too popular around there."

"No we're not, and I'm sorry I got you involved."

"Hey, Shannon, Vanessa and I owe you big time, and don't you worry about them filing harassment charges against me. From what Mac tells me, you all are closing in on these folks, and they're scared."

Shannon wasn't really surprised at the cult's reaction to Jackson's visit; if the tables had been turned, she'd have responded the same way. But she couldn't stop the small niggles of worry when it came to her young intern. These were bad people, capable of doing whatever it took to preserve the status quo. She spent another sleepless night and when she dragged herself into the office the next morning, was so tired she nearly missed the envelope that had been pushed under the door and now lay on the floor. Before she bent to retrieve it, she glanced down the street both ways, to see if whoever had delivered it was still in the area. But it was a little after seven and no one was around.

Closing the door behind her, she picked up the envelope and stared at it. Nothing bulky inside, nothing written on it. Just a plain white envelope. She slit it open and read the contents, a smile forming before she was a third of the way down the page.

Lupe had just declared that it was time to close up shop for the day when the bell over the door jangled and Shannon came hurrying through, all beaming triumph. At the sight of her, Mitch's heart gave a small lurch in his chest.

"We did it!"

This Shannon directed at Mac, who leaned on the edge of Lupe's desk, munching on a potato chip, and Lupe, who sat behind the desk, putting away a couple of files in a side drawer.

"What did we do?" Mac asked.

"We got Judge Montoya, bless his heart, to issue a freeze on JonahDawn's assets. The papers were served about an hour ago. JonahDawn is going down!" She pumped a fist in the air.

"Well done."

Shannon whirled around at the sound of his voice. He stood in front of the couch in the reception area.

Her first reaction was shock, followed immediately by pleasure, which gave way to an attempt to gather in the pleasure and present herself as pleased but distant. All of which Mitch observed in the space of a second, and it made him smile. She was right, she didn't lie very well; everything registered on that lively, open face of hers.

And God, how he'd missed her!

He walked over, stood gazing down on her, keeping his hands at his sides, even though he wanted to stroke her cheek, her neck, the ridge of her collarbones. "Hi Shannon," he said quietly.

She looked up, biting her lip before saying, "Mitch. What a surprise."

"I should have called first."

"No, really, it's okay. I've been so busy, I—" She left the sentence, which had a certain non-sequitur flair to it, unfinished.

She turned from him to the other two occupants of the room. "Lupe Delgado, Mac Marshall, meet Mitchell Connor, our client."

"We've already met," Mac said, his tone neutral. Mitch got the impression he was being sized up, approval being withheld until further investigation.

Lupe nodded, warmer, more pleased. "He's been waiting for you for hours. We were going to call you to tell you he was here but he insisted we not bother you."

She whirled around, a frown between her brows. "Why wouldn't you bother me?"

"I wanted to surprise you." He felt somewhat foolish now for the impulse.

"Well, that you did." She chuckled. "Nearly gave me a heart attack." She grabbed his hand and began leading him toward the rear of the storefront. "Come into my office. Tell me how you are, what's been going on?"

What had been going on? More than he could express at the moment, for sure.

The minute Mitch had returned to New Hampshire, he'd attacked the mess his extended absence had caused. Knowing there was only a short window of opportunity in which to put the pieces back together, he worked sixteen to eighteen hours at a pop, bringing himself up to speed on finances and personnel. He met daily with his executive staff, most of whom were still—amazingly enough—with the company. He issued bonuses to key employees, soothed hurt feelings, put out fires, made phone calls to banks, accountants, lawyers. He instructed his own personal lawyer to contest any claim made by JonahDawn on Joan's estate. It had already been done, he was told, and welcome home. In public, he presented a persona that was sharp, in charge, responsible, reliable and in no danger of disappearing again. The old Mitchell Connor, CEO, his demeanor said firmly, was back.

Privately, he continued to suffer. Sleep was fitful; he would return from a full day at his business consumed with new layers of guilt for those he'd let down on top of the previous layers of responsibility he felt for the deaths of Joan and Jamie. Sometimes he thought he couldn't bear another moment of missing his little boy. When he was checked out by his doctor, who suggested he take antidepressant medication to help him through a difficult time, he declined; he wanted nothing to blunt his feelings. It was his punishment and he would see it all the way through.

He also wanted nothing to blunt his intention to destroy Jonah and Aurora Denton. If his thirst for revenge had been put on simmer, every time he pictured Jamie's small casket, or that first sight of his lifeless body in the morgue, it fed the fire, kept it burning.

He didn't go home, not once. Even with his need to punish himself, he couldn't bear to face it, especially

Jamie's room. He stayed at a hotel, had his things brought over. He did some reading on the stages of mourning and he understood that the blackness of his mood wouldn't last forever, that at some point there would be acceptance, a lightening of the pain. But for the present, it continued to infuse every minute he was alone.

He thought often of Shannon, not just of that last night, but of all the time spent with her. It had been days only, but they'd been full days. They'd covered a hell of a lot of territory in that short time, and he'd wound up feeling as close, as connected, as he'd ever felt with anyone in his life. If she were with him now, he knew, she would alleviate some of his darkness, the way she had back in L.A. It was simply part of her caretaker/healer nature to function as sun breaking through storm clouds, bringing relief and light.

But he was still convinced that telling her they had no future was the right thing to do. He had no heart to give to anyone. Still, the more he thought about her, the more he missed her. There were the e-mails, of course, keeping him up to speed on the legal attack on JonahDawn, but he didn't call her nor did she call him. He needed to focus on his business, needed to get through this time, as he had gotten through all the difficult times of his life, alone.

By the end of the third week, the missing her had grown stronger than the need to be alone, and he'd arranged for a quick three-day trip back to the West Coast. Now here he was, and he could say none of that at the moment.

He tugged at her hand, so she'd stop moving. "Look, I don't want to interfere with your workday, you're so obviously busy."

"Darn right we are." She grinned up at him. "Remember my intern, Callie? Hereafter referred to as Super-Spy? She managed to slip us the numbers of a couple of private accounts held by Jonah and Aurora Denton, not to mention the passwords of some secret computer files, and have we been having the best time!" Her hand flew to her mouth, covering it, her eyes wide. "Ohmygod, that should not have been said out loud, in case you're ever called to testify against me."

"Aren't you protected by lawyer-client confidentiality?" he asked with a smile. "Or does that only go one way?"

"Unfortunately." She shook her head. "I can't believe I just did that. I mean, I really blew it."

"Not to worry. I have a little trouble with my memory, don't forget. Amnesia victim, blow to the head. And right now I don't recall anything you just said, except I'm really pleased with whatever progress you've made and I'd like to hear all about it. Dinner tonight?"

He saw the rush of pleasure on her face again, which definitely warmed him. *She* warmed him, had from the beginning, found the icy places inside him and melted them.

"Sure," she said, affecting nonchalance, he assumed for the sake of her office staff. "Tell me where and when?"

"Well, we—"

The bell over the door jangled again and everyone turned at once to see who the newcomer was. A man stood in the open doorway. If the look of fury on his face could have had the power to kill, they would all be goners by now.

It was Jonah Denton.

At the sight of him a red haze gathered in front of Mitch's eyes; his own, equally fierce rage burst into flame inside him.

"You!" Denton pointed at Shannon. "I warned you, didn't I? You think you can get away with what you're doing? Do you have any idea who you're dealing with?"

Mac got to his feet while Shannon, ever the fearless warrior, faced their visitor, head-on. "Why if it isn't the 'blessed Father' himself. Come to pay us a little visit, have you?"

The look on Denton's face, which Mitch didn't think could get any stormier, did so, and he realized the man had snapped. Mitch found his gaze quickly shifting to Denton's hands, on the lookout for a sudden movement that might produce a gun. Without thinking, Mitch stepped in front of Shannon, shielding her, even as she protested, "Hey!" from behind him.

Thrusting his hands behind him, momentarily imprisoning her, he said, "Hello, Jonah. Remember me?"

Jonah, who had been so focused on Shannon nothing much else had registered, took a look at him. At first, his gaze narrowed and he seemed momentarily confused.

Then, as realization dawned, his face expressed shock and dismay. "Why are you here? I read that you're—"

"Safely tucked away in New Hampshire?"

The other man recovered quickly. "No, I— What are you doing here?" he repeated, a wary, caged look on his face.

"Perhaps you haven't been officially introduced?" Shannon said, stepping out from behind him. "I believe you met the first time when my client looked somewhat different. Jonah Denton, meet Mitchell Connor."

"Client?"

Mitch let Shannon's use of the word hang in the air for a moment before saying, "As in the wrongful death lawsuit against you and Aurora on behalf of my late wife, Joan, and my son, Jamie."

"Or haven't you gotten those particular papers from your lawyer yet?" Shannon asked. "There's been so many, some may have been lost in transit."

Jonah Denton's cheek twitched as he tried to school his face to behave. "Wrongful death? Oh, no. I mean, we were so very sorry to hear—"

Mitch was the one who snapped then. Fury—deep and dark and primal—erupted inside him. He lunged at Denton, clamped his hands around his neck, and squeezed. "You killed them, you son of a bitch. My little boy is dead because of you."

Eyes wide with fear, Jonah tore at Mitch's wrists with his hands, but he was no match for the ferocity of the attack.

Through the haze of red in front of his eyes and filling his head, Mitch heard voices yelling at him, but they seemed to be coming from a distance. Hands grabbed at his arms, tugged at them, urging him to stop.

"Mitch, no!"

"Connor, cut it out."

"Dios mio."

But he couldn't and wouldn't stop. This man had to pay. Jonah Denton had to die.

For what seemed like long moments, Shannon felt paralyzed, helpless in the face of so much brute force. The expression on Mitch's face was savage; it was obvious he intended nothing less than to end Jonah's life. Not that she would weep for too long if that happened, but if it meant Mitch serving jail time and pretty much ruining his life, then no. Not acceptable.

While Mac, having inserted a shoulder between the two men, was trying to push them apart, Shannon planted herself behind Mitch, pulling at his belt and yelling for him to stop. But neither she nor Mac were successful; Jonah's face grew redder and redder, his eyes looking as if they were about to pop out of his head.

Then Louis stepped into the room, out of breath as though he'd been running. He quickly assessed the situation and, using his superior brute strength, managed to break Mitch's grip on Jonah's neck, although not without a struggle.

Jonah fell to the floor, gasping for breath, clutching his throat with one hand and pointing at Mitch with the other. "Louis," he said, his voice reduced to a rasp, "he tried to kill me."

"Yes, Father. I saw."

Mac continued to hold a struggling Mitch by the arms; even so, to Shannon, he appeared only slightly less threatening than he had moments ago. "Louis," Mitch said harshly. "It was you. You're the one who beat me up, left me for dead."

The accusation seemed to take the beefy young man by surprise, but, like Jonah before him, he soon recognized in the well-groomed man from last week's headlines the homeless person who had been at the compound a few weeks before. His mouth opened, as though he were about to speak, then he shook his head, signaling he'd changed his mind.

Instead, he pulled Jonah to his feet. "I think we better leave, Father," he said heavily. "It was not a good idea to come here. Violence is not the Bahlindulah way."

If she had thought the young man capable of irony, Shannon would have sworn she'd just heard it in his tone.

One brawny arm slung around Jonah's shoulders for support, Louis helped him out the door. At the last moment, he angled his head around, met Shannon's gaze and mouthed some words. Then he and Denton shuffled off, turning right as they cleared the doorway.

As the door shut behind them, Mac asked, "What did he say, Shannon?"

She stood, stock-still and terrified to the very depths of her being. "I'm pretty sure he said, 'Get Callie out.'"

From behind Mitch, Mac asked, "Are you sure?"

"Not entirely, but eighty percent."

"Wishful thinking?"

Shannon's answer was indignant. "Why would I wish for that?"

Mitch finally found his voice. "I saw it, too," he said, trying to catch his breath. "And, by the way, you can release me now."

"Oh." Mac dropped his hold on Mitch's arms. "Sorry, man."

"It's okay." He rotated his shoulders, trying to loosen up his muscles. Not just out of breath but depleted, all over. And numb inside.

The bell over the door jangled once again, signaling the arrival of yet one more newcomer. Mitch felt himself tensing up again as everyone in the room turned to see who it was.

A tall, blond woman, thirtyish and dressed in loose plaid slacks, clogs and a cropped sweater, swept in, her arms filled with plants. "Oh, goody," she said with a smile that reminded Mitch of Shannon's, "you're all still here."

She set the plants down carefully on the coffee table, then plucked off one yellowing leaf. "I was afraid I was too late."

When there was no response, she turned around to face the group and stood, a puzzled expression replacing the cheerful smile of a moment earlier. "What? What's up?"

"Nothing that concerns you, Carm," Shannon said.

"Don't use that big-sister tone on me, Shannon. What is it?" One by one she made eye contact with the rest of the room's occupants. "Mac? Lupe?" When her gaze landed on Mitch, she said, "And who are you?"

"Mitchell Connor." His fists were clenched, he realized, and he unclenched them, told his body to ease up on the alert status. He reached out his hand and she shook it.

"You're the one in the papers last week," Shannon's sister said, a smile of excitement on her pretty, soft face. "That missing big-shot business guy."

"He's my client," Shannon said, flicking a quick glance at him before looking away. "Mitch, this is Carmen, my nosy baby sister."

"I figured."

"Wow," Carmen said. "It's really cool to meet you."

Again, she looked from Mac to Shannon, Lupe to Mitch. Hands on hips, she declared, "Okay, enough. Fill me in."

"Carmen," Shannon said warningly.

"Shannon." Carmen mocked her sister's tone. "I'm not moving until I hear the story. All of it."

With a loud sigh, Shannon started in on the tale. "You ever hear of a group named JonahDawn…?"

Mac went over to his desk, got out a round brown bottle and paper cup, made eye contact with Mitch and jerked his head in the direction of Shannon's office, indicating he was to follow him. Mitch did so, wondering how a person could feel so alternately shut down and ready to fight to the death. It wreaked havoc on his insides.

Inside the office, he lowered himself onto the settee in one corner of the office, while Mac sat on a small adjacent armchair.

"How you holding up?"

Grateful for the kindness in the other man's voice, Mitch offered a small smile. "Wiped out. And I guess a little shaky."

Mac poured him a generous shot from the bottle, which was marked Brandy. "Here, slug it down."

He took it and did as he was told. The warmth hit his system immediately, soothing him and waking him up at the same time. He sat back, closed his eyes. "Thanks."

A comfortable silence passed between the two men before Mitch opened his eyes again, murmuring, "I've never felt like that in my life. Ever."

"Yeah. The rage to kill." Mac shook his head. "It's pretty powerful stuff."

"Have you ever felt it?"

"Too many times to count. I was a cop for twenty-five years, an alcoholic longer than that. And the combination of booze and the power to shoot a weapon was lethal, trust me. My rage meter was off the scale. I killed two men in the line of duty, and I'm not sure, even to this day, that their deaths were necessary, even though they were armed and dangerous. The second time scared the piss out of me, so I finally gave up the booze. But one thing I will tell you, man, is that after you've taken a human life, you're never the same again. Never. Life is too damn precious and if you rob someone of their chance to live it, well, it changes you." He paused before saying, "The good news is I've been clean and sober for thirteen years now, and my rage meter is under control."

"Impressive. But why keep a bottle of brandy in your desk?"

"For emergencies. For others, I mean. And to remind me not to go there again."

Mitch thought about this, then gave a mirthless chuckle. "I don't have alcohol as an excuse."

"No, but you got grief. And a need to get even. It floods your system same way the booze does."

Mitch lowered his head, put his hands over his face. "I nearly killed him."

"But you didn't."

"Only because all of you were there preventing me from carrying out my plan."

"Good thing for him," Mac said with a small smile.

"I just…snapped. All I could think of was that he had to die."

Again, the two men sat in thoughtful silence. The phone rang in the outer office and someone answered it. Behind the closed door Mitch could hear the voices of Shannon and her sister but couldn't make out the words.

"Shannon said something a while ago," he told Mac,

"and I didn't want to hear it, but I think she was right. She said that I was under the illusion that revenge would bring my son, Jamie, back. That whatever I do I can't reverse the fact that he's gone. Forever. I know that, of course, intellectually. Nothing will." The sadness filled his chest cavity then. "I hate this feeling, this…being powerless to stop the pain."

"Grief," Mac said simply. "It takes a long time to get to the other side. Been there myself. I know."

"I'd like there to be a shortcut."

"Yeah. But there isn't one. Not if the person who's gone meant a lot. They deserve all the time it takes."

The door was flung open and female energy entered the room in the person of the Coyle sisters. Shannon was just at the end of the story, which Carmen kept interrupting with questions. Mitch watched them, one short, one tall, one dark-haired, one blond. But with the same eyes, eyebrows and that open, generous smile. They'd also apparently each inherited the trait of extreme animation, expressive hands and faces. Not an ounce of subtlety about either of them.

They were close, there was no escaping it. Warm and gregarious. They'd grown up in a family that had nurtured all of those qualities. Unlike his own, unlike Joan's, and, sadly, unlike the family he'd tried to make with Joan and Jamie. There had been very little display—his entire life, he realized—of honest, genuine affection.

Except with Jamie.

An image of his son's round, innocent face floated into Mitch's brain, and he half expected to hear the familiar "Help me, Daddy" refrain. But he didn't. In fact, he hadn't heard it for a few days.

Was Jamie fading from his memory already? No. Of course not. But maybe some of his guilt was? He knew that was what the voice represented. Would the guilt pass as time went on, the way grief was supposed to?

Too much self-reflection, he thought, and downed the rest of his brandy. His head still hurt from the adrenaline rush he'd experienced trying to kill Jonah, but he felt less chilled now, and less exhausted. Less distant.

He rose from the settee, saying, "Would either of you like to sit?"

Shannon, who was pacing, glanced at him briefly, said, "Can't," and went back to pacing. Carmen perched a hip on the edge of Shannon's desk, saying, "No thanks."

So Mitch sat back down and joined Mac and Carmen in watching an agitated Shannon pace while she thought out loud. "We have to get Callie out of there."

The intercom buzzed. Shannon stopped, pressed the speaker button. "Yes, Lupe?"

"Can you see a client tomorrow? It's Mrs. Foster with the cat litter in the toilet thing."

Shannon raised her eyes to the heavens, then said, "Make it for the following day, all right? In fact, call whoever is coming in tomorrow and put them off. Thanks, Lupe. And you need to go home."

"When you do, I will."

Shannon pressed the speaker off button and resumed her pacing. "Ideas, people. We need to take action."

"A warrant?" Carmen suggested.

"It will take too long. Besides, we don't have any real, tangible evidence that anything bad is being done to her. Just some words I thought I saw being mouthed silently by a young man who is definitely not all there upstairs. No judge will go for it."

Back and forth, back and forth she went. Shannon in motion was a wonder to behold.

"I can call Jackson, see what he thinks," Mac said.

"I don't want to impose on him any more unless we have something solid he can act on. I mean we can't just bust in there, not that I wouldn't do it, but there's the gate and the alarm system and who knows where Callie is, and by the time we found her, they would be counterattacking." She stopped, worried her bottom lip. "We need to do something. Now."

Mac shook his head. "Shannon, it ain't gonna happen tonight, and you know it."

As though she hadn't heard him, she mused, "Maybe we could stage a kidnapping. Hire a professional. How in the world do you find a professional kidnapper? Not by advertising on the Internet," she said dryly. "What we need is a commando force or a SWAT team."

"You've been watching too much TV again," Mac

observed. "And tell me, why are you listening to what Louis said? Wouldn't Callie have gotten out by now if she thought she was in danger?"

"What if she can't?" Again she stopped pacing, got a look of concentration on her face. "How can we contact Louis?"

"Can't you call up there, ask for him?" Carmen suggested.

"Not as myself, no. It will arouse suspicion. Maybe you could, Carm. I don't know, pretend you're—"

"Sorry," Mac interrupted. "I'm thinking if he is on our side, the less you involve Louis right now, the better it will be for Callie. We don't need to shine any kind of spotlight on him."

"Yeah." Suddenly, Shannon got a look of wonder on her face. "Do you think he's the one who has her cell phone? The one who sent the SOS?"

What cell phone, what SOS? Mitch wondered, having been able to follow the conversation up to now.

"He's keeping it hidden I'll bet," Shannon was saying. "Where's my purse?"

"I think you left it out in the waiting room," he said.

It was the first time Mitch had opened his mouth in a while and Shannon flicked a glance at him, startled, as though she'd forgotten he was there. Then she nodded. "Thanks. And by the way, we have to talk," she added, scurrying out to the reception area.

Mitch looked from Carmen to Mac. "Is she like this often?"

Carmen grinned. "Shannon's in the zone, we used to say at home. She thinks better when she's moving."

The object of their discussion came bustling back into the room, fishing around in her purse before she produced her cell phone. They all watched as she hit a button, listened, then said, "Sorry. Wrong number."

She set the phone down, a thoughtful expression on her face as she murmured, "Voice mail picked up."

Carmen asked, "Why didn't you leave a message?"

"In case Louis isn't the one who has it and I'm completely off base here. Heck, it could be anyone up there. You should see them, Carm, all the JonahDawn converts. With their shaved heads and white robes, like zombies out of some horror flick. Gives me the creeps just thinking about them." Back to pacing. "How can we get in there as soon as possible?"

"A disguise?" Carmen offered.

Shannon stopped, considered it. "Could work. I could pretend to be someone else, get past the gate that way."

"Posing as who or what?" Mitch asked, joining in the discussion for the first time because he was becoming alarmed at the direction of her thoughts.

"No way, Counselor." Mac's pronouncement was curt and definite.

"Why not?" Shannon glared at him. "I can be an old lady with a wig, granny glasses, makeup."

"Your height. Your personality. You're not a good enough actress to cover that up."

"Who says?"

"Actress!" Carmen sprang up from her perch and headed for the door. "We have an actress, right outside the front door."

"Excuse me?"

"Remember that homeless lady, Gidget, who used to live in the alleyway near my old place? Where I lived before J.R. and I got married? She had that dog, Bonzo?"

Gidget? Bonzo? Mitch felt thoroughly out of the loop.

"Gidget," Shannon said, nodding. "Little white-haired lady. Missing some teeth. Always has her shopping cart with her."

"She used to be an actress in the movies," Carmen explained, "before she had a breakdown. The poor thing can't stand to be inside four walls anymore. She has severe claustrophobia. But I've hired her, well, part-time. She helps with the outdoor section at our Culver City nursery. Anyway, she's waiting outside for me right now. I'll go get her."

She stopped, turned back to them. "Or, rather, we'd all better go to her. She won't come in." Carmen grinned again. "Amazing how life just works out, isn't it? Come on, all of you. Come meet Gidget."

Mitch stayed where he was, watching as they all trooped out. He felt like an outsider, which of course he was. He opened the brandy bottle and poured himself another healthy amount, then slugged it down.

The best laid plans, as the saying went. Instead of accomplishing what he'd come back to L.A. for, which was to see Shannon, and then to— What? He hadn't gotten that far. Because, within one minute of setting eyes on her, he'd nearly killed a man.

She'd witnessed the whole thing and was now treating him either as someone about whom she'd just found something distasteful...or as an afterthought.

Neither fit his pictures of what he'd planned. He felt lost, adrift.

Alone.

Chapter 10

Mind racing with all the plans for the morning, Shannon headed back to her office to find Mitch still sitting on the small sofa, staring off into space.

"There you are," she said with as much cheer as she could manage. "Are you doing okay?"

He nodded, raising a paper cup. "Brandy helps," he said. "So what's the plan?"

She chewed her bottom lip. "We have to wait for morning. I wanted to storm the place tonight, but I got voted down. Which, I know, is the logical thing to do, but I'm not feeling very logical at the moment." She tried to shrug it off. "Anyhow, tomorrow's one of the days JonahDawn rounds up the homeless, buses them

up to the compound and feeds them. Gidget will be part
of that, slip a note to Louis to have Callie by the gate
when they take them back. Then she'll create a diver-
sion as the gate is being opened, and if Louis got the
note and if Callie is able or willing to take part in this
whole rescue thing, she'll slip out, and we'll pick her
up. A big 'if' all around. But it's the best we could
come up with."

"I'd like to help."

She didn't know how to answer that one, so she
stared at him for a moment while she gathered her
thoughts. This was not the time for one of her tell-the-
truth-or-be-damned outbursts, even she knew that.

Mitch was the one who filled the silence. "But it's
probably better if I stay on the sidelines?"

She walked over to her desk, boosted herself onto it.
"That was pretty scary, what happened with Jonah."

"Yeah."

"Understandable, though."

He raised and lowered a shoulder. "Nice of you to say."

"I mean I've personally never gotten so close to
losing it before, but it's that instinct we all have in us.
'You hurt what's mine and you're dead' kind of thing."

"I guess." He shook his head, obviously working
something through. "I'm a grown-up, responsible,
rational man and I felt like an animal. I still want him
to die, Shannon, and that's the truth." He expelled a
breath, then leaned his head back against the couch and
went on thoughtfully. "See, I thought about all of this

while I was back east. I had a plan. Murdering a murderer is not only frowned on by society, it isn't in my best interests. I decided it would be more satisfactory to shut them down, throw them in jail. Make them suffer, for years and years on end. I was willing to wait, to go through whatever it took, but they would pay. It was to be my mission."

He opened his eyes, sat up straight and made eye contact with her. "And then, in one insane moment, all that careful planning flew out the window. I wish I could say I'm sorry I did it, but I'm not. I am sorry you had to see it."

So was she. She'd been terrified of that Mitch, that was the truth. It moved him into a category of potentially dangerous men, putting the lie to her previous certainty that he would not be a member of that group.

But she didn't want to deal with it anymore. "So, what about your business?"

The change of subject did what she'd intended, got them onto safer ground. "I've set the wheels in motion to sell it. We're breaking it up into smaller parts, I'll maintain some interest in it. It's complicated, but no one will suffer much. It feels like the right thing to do. There's nothing for me there, not anymore."

"Oh?" A little flare of hope rose inside her. "Well, if you think that's best," she said, all the while thinking, If there's nothing for you there, what about here? Did you come back to see me, to be with me? And why didn't you call?

Again, miracle of miracles, she actually kept her inner monologue to herself. The man did not need her little female insecurities at this moment; they seemed so trivial in the face of his violent outburst, not to mention the upcoming, hoped-for rescue of her intern.

"So that's the reason you came back?" It just popped out of her mouth, even as she had decided it shouldn't. "To get even?"

Blatant fishing, Shannon. You should be ashamed of yourself.

His gaze was solemn. "One of them. And to get you to back off of this case because I realized I was afraid for you. These people are dangerous."

"Gee, really?"

"Seriously Shannon." He moved so he was sitting on the very edge of the couch now, elbows resting on his knees, his hands clasped tightly between them. "I'm assuming from what Jonah said that you've already been threatened by them. Isn't that enough? For God's sake, distance yourself. Let the others do whatever they have to in the morning to get your intern away from them, but you need to stay clear of the compound. And then, when all that's over, back off. Please. Let me hire a different law firm, get some security professionals on the case. By putting yourself front and center like this, you're making yourself a target. This is my fight, not yours."

She felt her temper rising. "Hold it—"

He didn't let her finish. "Mine and mine alone. If you

wound up dead, like Joan and Jamie, I'd never forgive myself. Never."

Okay, now she was really getting angry. "You're not responsible for me. Do you hear me? This isn't about you, Mitch. Or not only about you. I'm representing other clients in this matter as well as you, remember? It's both our fight. I was after JonahDawn before I met you and I'll be after them until they're history."

He jumped up, moved toward her. "And what if you get killed along the way?"

She jutted her chin out. "I can take care of myself."

"Really? What, did you take a couple of self-defense classes? You know to go for the eyes or the groin? Big deal. You weigh, what? A hundred pounds? To someone like Louis, that's like flicking off a fly."

That did it! Anger made her hop off the desk, which turned out to be not such a great idea. Face-to-face, Mitch was over a foot taller than her, so it was more of a face-to-lower-chest thing. If she'd ever cursed her height before in her life, she was double cursing it now.

Even so, she glared up at him, pointed her index finger at his chest and stabbed him with it, saying, "Don't you dare do that to me. Don't belittle me. Don't make me the helpless woman, unable to cope with the bad men."

He grabbed her weapon hand. "Don't you get it? If something happened to you, I'd want to die."

"Being a little dramatic here, aren't we?"

"No, just telling the truth." He dropped her hand and

took her by the shoulders. "I care about you, Shannon. A lot. Too much. More than I deserve to."

He shook her again, then with a curse, dropped his grip on her shoulders, making her sag back against the desk, while he turned and walked away.

She got it then, got that he was scared, not just for her, but about his *feelings* for her.

"Hey, Mitch," she said softly to his back. "It's okay. Really it is."

He said nothing. She stared at his back, studied it, considered him. What a complicated man. So many devils driving him.

But he cared about her. He did. She'd seen it in the way he'd looked at her, seen it shining from those deep, haunted, beautiful silver eyes of his. Felt it in the passion of his fear for her. And as ludicrous as it was— coming on top of her worries about Callie and her lack of sleep and the piles and piles of work she had stacked on her desk, and yes, some fear of Jonah Denton and the rage she'd seen in his eyes—it made her glow inside.

He cared.

She was in love with him, and he cared.

He was filled with ghosts and guilt and in mourning and driven by a need for revenge.

And he cared.

Not quite love yet, but on the road to it.

Finally, he turned around, shook his head with exasperation. "I don't know what to do with you,

Shannon, but I am worried about you, I will continue to worry about you. You don't like it? Tough."

She sighed. "Okay, if it makes you feel better, worry away. We can have a chain, you worry about me, I'll worry about Callie. Because if anything happens to her, I'll never forgive myself."

"But wasn't she the one who volunteered? You didn't send her in, did you?"

"No, I tried to argue her out of it."

"So why are you to blame?"

"Because I am. She admired me. Wanted to be as brave as I was. Brave, right. It's all a crock."

Again, he moved toward her, framed her face with his hands. "This isn't your fault."

"Pot calling the kettle black."

One side of his mouth curved up in a smile. "Impasse, I'm thinking."

"And I'm agreeing."

He dropped his hands from her face, put his arms around her waist. "Come have dinner with me."

"I can't eat. I'm too anxious. I could keep you company, I guess."

"Forget dinner. Come to my hotel, spend the night with me. I think I can probably calm you down." Now his smile was seductive, and oh, so tempting.

"Can't." Regret filled her. "We're all taking turns babysitting Gidget, to make sure she doesn't change her mind. We're camping out at the nursery."

"Camping out?"

"Yeah. Sleeping bags, tents, the whole thing. She likes that, Gidget does. I have never been into that sort of thing myself."

"Mac, too?"

She nodded. "He's the one with the sleeping bags."

"All right, then. As long as he's there with you, I'll feel better. But I would like to help in the morning. If nothing else, I intend to keep you from getting into trouble."

"Come by at six. It's Kurtz Nurseries in Culver City. If we can use you, we will. But, Mitch, seriously now, if you think you're going to lose it again, please stay away."

She wondered if her words would sting, but he nodded, not in the least bit defensive. "Makes sense. And now I'm going to walk you to your car."

"I'm going to let you. I wouldn't even turn down a kiss or three before I have to leave."

"I just might be able to comply."

It went pretty much as planned, with some improvisation along the way. The entire story in all its details wouldn't be known to Shannon and Mitch until much later, but it began with the fact that Gidget wouldn't ride the bus, so Carmen drove her and Bonzo most of the way up to the compound in one of the nursery's open pickup trucks. Mac, Shannon and Mitch followed in the SUV Mitch had rented. It was the largest of all their cars, and they figured if Callie needed a place to stretch out, or if, by some chance, Louis came along, there'd be enough room.

Both vehicles parked down the road and out of sight of the compound, in a small neighborhood park. When the bus carrying that morning's load of street people passed by, Gidget trotted up the hill behind it. When the bus was waved through she was to do the same, as though she'd walked all the way and expected her breakfast. Most likely no one would question her; if central casting had put out a call for an elderly homeless woman, she would have been their number-one pick.

Even partway down the hill, and out of sight of the compound, being this near the JonahDawn compound made Mitch's insides roil, but he counseled himself to be calm. He was here for Shannon, not for himself. She needed to be the focus of his attention. Plenty of time to deal with his need to punish Jonah down the road.

It was a good two hours before the exit part of the plan would happen and Shannon spent the time pacing, worrying out loud. Once in a while, Carmen drew her to the side, engaged her in little tête-à-têtes intended to take her mind off what was happening: what the baby in her uterus looked like now, how the Kurtz Nurseries were expanding, how Mom had called her to tell her she'd actually gone out on her first date since Dad had died.

In between these bursts of conversation, Shannon would return to her pacing. Mac and Mitch exchanged the occasional male-to-male observation about women and their nerves, but mostly they were silent.

Time passed. As Carmen was the only one of them who had never been to the compound and had no history with JonahDawn, she was the one who could stroll by the gate and peer in with impunity. So, in between chatting with Shannon, she took Bonzo on his leash, and did just that, hoping for a glimpse of Louis, who had been described to her in detail, or seeing if Callie had planted herself in the shrubbery.

No sightings of either of them, she reported on her return from the first foray into enemy territory.

The four of them, Shannon had to acknowledge, were completely out of the loop where they were, hoping that Gidget would come through for them but knowing that they were basically at the mercy of a homeless, claustrophobic, often-paranoid aging actress and her moods. Not a comforting thought in the least.

The fourth time Carmen made her expedition she came running back to report that breakfast was over and the bus was being loaded up again. When she took off again, Shannon started to run after her.

Mitch grabbed her, pulled her back behind a thick tree trunk. "Don't even think about it."

"I'll hide in the bushes. No one will see me."

"Not going to happen, Shannon."

"But what if it gets all screwed up?"

"If you show your face, you might be the one to screw it up."

"God! I can't stand this waiting!"

An earsplitting scream filled the air, then another, shattering the quiet of the morning.

Mac, Shannon and Mitch exchanged glances, then they smiled. Part B of the plan had just gone into effect. Gidget had told them that she'd been in two low-budget horror films and that she'd been hired because she was one of the best screamers in L.A. Shannon had to admit that what she was hearing now were extremely effective screams of terror, most definitely coming from the direction of the castle.

That meant that the bus had approached the gate, the gate was open, and Gidget was running away from the bus, back toward the castle and around to the rear; in theory, her screams would draw all attention in the opposite direction, away from the gate area, most likely even lure the guard from the gatehouse, giving Callie a chance to slip through the open gate undetected.

It was a desperate, insane plan, Shannon realized now, wondering how in the world she'd let Carmen talk her into it. She was some kind of fool. She clung silently to Mitch's arm, waiting to find out if, by some miracle, Callie would appear.

And then, with the screams getting farther and farther away, Carmen appeared, her arm around a weeping Callie. Shannon's heart soared with gratitude. As she spirited her intern into the waiting SUV and got her settled in the back, the screams at the castle ceased as abruptly as they had started. The next part of the plan was for Gidget to shake her head, look around, smile at everyone and act as if nothing had happened, just another schizoid event among so many others.

She would then exit in the wake of the bus, the way she'd come in. If worse came to worse and they called an ambulance for her, Carmen was listed as Gidget's contact and responsible party, so either way, Gidget would be back under the stars tonight, Bonzo at her side.

Mitch, with Shannon in the rear seat, her arm around Callie, started up the engine. Mac appeared at the driver's side window. "Hey, you okay, Callie?"

Callie managed to nod. "I'll be fine," she said, her voice wobbly, then instantly went back to sobbing.

Mac shot her a worried look, then said to Mitch and Shannon, "That was some Academy Award–winning performance back there, huh? Gidget's strolling down the road right now, calm as you please, like nothing's wrong. Carmen and I will drive her back in the pickup. You get going. Call you later, Shannon."

As they headed back toward Venice, Shannon comforted Callie as best she could, holding her, rocking her. She was even thinner than she'd been before; she was all bones and very little flesh. "You'll feel better when you rest. We need to get some food into you." She dug around in her purse, found an energy bar, unwrapped it and handed it to Callie. The young woman gobbled it up so fast, Shannon was worried she'd be sick.

"Where are we taking her?" Mitch asked, making

eye contact with Shannon in the rearview mirror. "Not to your place. It's the first place they'll look."

"I know. We're going to Lupe's."

"Smart."

Shannon gave him directions and continued to hug Callie and murmur soothing words to her.

At the small house in Mar Vista, Lupe was all warm, motherly readiness. "Come," she told Callie. "I have a bed ready for you. I made good, warm soup, with little meatballs in it."

"Maybe later, Lupe," Callie managed to say. "I have to lie down."

Mitch was shown to a coffeepot and fresh muffins in the kitchen, then Lupe and Shannon helped Callie to a cozy bedroom and into a bed covered with handmade quilts.

"Stay," the young woman told Shannon, as she and Lupe made to leave. "Please. I need to tell you."

"Later, Callie. You should rest."

"No. Now. Before I sleep. Please."

"You stay with her," Lupe said. "I will keep your friend company. It will be my pleasure to visit with such a beautiful man," she added with a twinkle in her eye.

Shannon sat on the bed and took Callie's thin, cold hand in hers. "Didn't they feed you?" she asked, and listened while Callie spoke, sometimes quickly, sometimes taking a moment to find a word or to wipe away a tear.

If she was even thinner than normal, it was because

she'd stopped eating a few days ago when she'd found out her food was being drugged. She'd been horrified, but apparently the Dentons had targeted her as the culprit who'd managed to hack into the computer and discover the secret bank accounts. They were planning on arranging a little "accidental overdose" to happen to her.

Shannon was horrified, but kept her mouth shut and just listened as Callie spewed. In the beginning, when she'd first gone "undercover," it had been kind of fun, acting, getting into the chanting and being one of Jonah's "daughters." But it was Aurora, not Jonah, who'd begun to scare her. "I'm pretty sure she's the one who has my cell phone and sent the SOS."

"Why?"

"She wanted to see you, face-to-face, see the lawyer lady Jonah disliked so. That's what Louis thinks, anyway. Aurora's freaky. I think she may be a witch," she told Shannon, her eyes wide in her narrow face.

"You believe in that stuff?"

"I never did before. I'm not so sure now."

It was Louis who had helped her get into the office to get the account numbers, Louis who'd begun to look out for her, who had let her know she was in danger. "He's so sweet," she said earnestly. "Really. Inside, I mean."

"Sweet or no, Callie, Mitch is pretty sure he's the one who beat him up."

"He was. He's slow, his brain doesn't always work

really well and they found out early on how to manipulate him. They convinced him that Mr. Connor was a devil sent to destroy the Bahlindulah principles, and that Louis would become a Select by taking care of this. Even then he couldn't kill Mr. Connor. He tried not to deliver any blows that would cause lasting damage. He hoped the beating would be enough to keep him away, which was what Jonah and Aurora wanted. But then Louis was guilty toward them and never told them what he'd done and was worrying about it all the time. He was split in two, and I think maybe his loyalty and devotion to them was starting to waver when I joined up."

"Did they know who Mitch really was?"

"Not at first but later on. They'd kept back some of Joan Connor's stuff and were looking through old pictures. There was one of Mr. Connor with a beard, like on a fishing trip or something. They made the connection then. Got scared, ordered Louis to kill him."

"Why did he drop Mitch off in front of my office?" Shannon asked.

"They told him to. They were really threatened by you, Shannon, from the first time you sent them a letter. They felt persecuted by you, wrongly, they kept insisting. I told them that you were some kind of avenger type and they were right and you were wrong. I had to make them think I was totally renouncing you. It worked, at first. I think I may have overdone it."

Her eyes as she spoke were huge, imploring, begging

Shannon's forgiveness. Gone completely was the A law student, the confident granddaughter of a con man; she was a shell of her former self, both on the outside and in.

Shannon patted her hand, smiled at her. "It's okay, you're safe now. But tell me, how did you get Louis to help you?"

"I think he fell a little bit in love with me. And that made him look at the Dentons in a different light."

She went on to tell Shannon how Louis had witnessed an already-unstable Joan Connor signing the new will while in a confused state. "But Louis wasn't responsible for their deaths, he swore to me, and I believe him. I think it was Aurora again. She has all these Eastern drugs and herbs, stuff that would probably not be picked up in normal tox screens. I think she gave them to Mr. Connor's wife and child. Aurora runs the show, but lets Jonah think he's in charge."

Shannon had so many questions to ask, details she was curious about, but Callie's eyes were beginning to close. "Rest now, sweetie," she said, rising. "We'll talk some more later."

Callie didn't answer; she was already sound asleep.

She should never have allowed her to go, Shannon chastised herself. It was her take-no-prisoners attitude when her rage at injustice was operating that was the cause of Callie's brush with death.

Deep in thought, she joined Lupe and Mitch in the small, bright kitchen.

Mitch looked up when Shannon walked in. She was frowning, thinking too hard. "You all right?" he asked, rising and making her sit in his chair, while he went and got himself a stool from the corner and perched on it.

"Yes. I'm okay. Poor Callie, poor baby. She's been through a nightmare."

Lupe poured her coffee, set fresh pumpkin muffins, Shannon's favorite, in front of her. Shannon drank the coffee but didn't touch the muffins. Uh-oh, Mitch thought. This was not good.

She related what Callie had told her, after which Mitch and she told Lupe all the details of the morning's successful escape plan. Then the three of them tossed ideas back and forth for a while about how JonahDawn operated. Finally, Shannon looked at her watch; they'd been here for hours. She sagged against Mitch, thoroughly exhausted. "I want to go home."

"I'm not sure your place is safe."

"It's a secure building. You need a key for the main door, another for the garage. I have a bolt on my door. I want to sleep in my own bed." She sounded like a cranky child, which made him smile.

"If you insist. I'm coming with you."

"I accept." She yawned, began to rise.

Her cell phone rang. It was Mac.

"Turn on the TV, Shannon. Channel Five. The Jonah-Dawn compound is on fire. It's huge!"

* * *

They spent more hours at Lupe's, glued to the television set. It was, indeed, a huge, raging conflagration, one that was difficult to bring under control and not helped by a sudden wind that had come up out of nowhere. Reporters on the scene quoted "unofficial sources" who said it had most likely been set on purpose and helped along by some incendiary accelerant, which was why it had spread so quickly. Whatever wasn't stone was burned to a crisp. Most of the compound's occupants were able to get out, some with severe burns, some completely unscathed, but still others—at least twenty poor souls at last count—had not made it.

As Shannon stared at the TV, horrified, she felt as if she were witnessing some kind of biblical Judgment Day. When she looked at Mitch, she knew he felt the same. No triumph. How could there be triumph when so many lives had been lost?

Identifications of the dead were slow in coming. In the late afternoon, with Callie still sleeping, Shannon told Lupe to call her when she woke up, then she and Mitch went back to her place.

Shannon sat up with a start. She was on her bed, fully clothed. Mitch lay beside her, also still in his clothes. It was morning. The TV was still on. They'd watched it into the night, even when regular programming had come on and all there had been about the JonahDawn fire were news updates.

What an awful night it had been. Bodies had been pulled from the embers for hours. IDs on the dead were being withheld pending notification of relatives, but Mac was able to get an unofficial list of the names and called her. The first one Shannon recognized was Louis Lee, and found herself saddened, sorry for the poor, slow young man. At least now she understood why Louis had told her to get Callie out. He had planned this murder-suicide by fire and had wanted her clear of any danger.

Aurora Denton was also ID'd, but there was no mention of Jonah yet. However, there were several still-unidentified bodies, and not all the names of those who had survived were known. It was assumed he was in one of those two groups.

Shannon talked to Callie several times. The young woman couldn't forgive herself. "I should have seen it coming. Louis. Meggie. Arnold. All those lives. It's all my fault. Me and my need to play hero."

Shannon did her best to talk her out of her self-flagellation, but it did no good. The final time Shannon hung up from the distraught young woman, she told Mitch, "Lupe says she's called Callie's mother, and she's on her way to get her and bring her home. I sure hope she gets here soon. She sounds suicidal."

"It's a tough burden to bear."

She shook her head. "What a sorry bunch we are. Callie blames herself for the fire, I blame myself for Callie. How are you doing with all your guilt?"

"Still alive and kicking."

"It sucks, big time. All of it."

Mitch had pulled her close, kissed the top of her head. By this time, they'd moved from the living room into the bedroom. They kept telling themselves they needed to turn the TV off, but neither of them made a move to do so. The fire was out and cleanup had begun. And still they'd watched. And fallen asleep watching.

Now, she gazed at Mitch, the strong planes of his face more pronounced in the morning light. He was sleeping soundly, and she thought of how peaceful he looked, and of how much she loved him. After all they'd been through since the evening before last, it was clear to her that each of them needed the other. They belonged together; she hoped he'd come to the same conclusion at some point down the road. Quietly, she got out of bed, changed out of her clothes and into a robe, and headed for the kitchen to put the coffee on.

Still not quite awake, she unfastened the safety chain on her front door, pulled it open and bent down to retrieve her morning paper.

She was shoved roughly back into her condo; a hand clamped over her mouth from behind before she could scream; the door kicked closed.

"Bitch," she heard a man say, then felt something sharp, like the point of a knife, on her neck, just below the ear. "Bitch," she heard again. It sounded halfway between a growl and a sob. "You killed her."

Jonah Denton's remains had not been identified because Jonah Denton was not dead.

Chapter 11

Furious thoughts zoomed through Shannon's head at the speed of light. Kick back with your foot, get him in the knees or the groin. Shove your elbow back. Put up a fight, resist, scream, stomp on the floor, throw yourself forward, go limp. All the things she'd been taught to do, but were useless with a knife at her neck.

"You killed my Aurora," he sobbed. "You killed my dream."

"I didn't set the fire, Jonah."

"No. Louis did it. Because you told him to."

"No, Jonah, that's not how it w—"

She halted in mid-sentence because he ran the knife down the side of her neck, not deep, but enough to draw blood. She felt the thick liquid drip down her neck; she was light-headed. Then he brought the knife around to the front of her throat, near the jugular. She began to shake uncontrollably, which made him chortle in triumph. Like one of those scenes in the movies, she thought wildly, where the bad guy loses it and does that evil-laugh thing, the one that grows and grows, echoing down the hallway.

Only this wasn't a movie and she was about to die.

Mitch nearly blew it. When he heard the door slam shut, he woke right up and was about to call out, "Shannon?" when something—Providence? His intuition? Sheer luck?—stopped him from doing so.

Instead, as quietly as he could, he got off the bed and crept to the door of the bedroom, keeping his body hidden, but venturing a peek. The sight that greeted him made his blood chill in his veins. Two figures were in profile. Jonah Denton had Shannon in a fierce grip, a knife at her throat.

Fear and fury rose, side by side, making his heart race. He clamped his jaw tight, told himself to get a grip. He needed a calm head; above all, he needed not to make a sound. Jonah began to drag Shannon toward the couch, which meant his back was now to Mitch. Moving quickly and stealthily, Mitch came up behind Jonah and went for the hand holding the knife. Even though he surprised Jonah, the other man didn't let go. They struggled, Mitch working to keep the knife away from Shannon, Jonah trying to stab her or Mitch with it.

There was an *umph* sound, and suddenly Shannon fell to the floor, blood pouring out of her side. That same red haze that had surrounded his head the day before came back with a vengeance, and Mitch wrestled the knife from Jonah and had him down, his knee on his chest, the knife poised above him, about to stab this sorry excuse for a human being again and again, until his life was extinguished.

"Mitch, don't."

Shannon, her hand over her wound, her face filled with pain, had managed to gasp out the request before passing out. But it was enough to still his hand for the moment.

Then Mac's words, also from yesterday, came to him: "After you've taken a human life, you're never the same again."

If he crossed that line, he would change irrevocably, and he had a feeling that wouldn't be a good thing for his peace of mind. Or for his future with Shannon.

Instead, he threw the knife across the room and punched Jonah, hard, in the face, twice, which was enough to knock him out. His knuckles hurt but it had been more than worth it. He ran for the phone, contacted 911, then got down on his knees next to Shannon and went to work staunching the flow of blood from her side.

It was Mitch's turn to pace now. He and Mac, Carmen and her husband J.R.—who was apparently another of Shannon's volunteers at the Last House on the Block—were in the waiting room of the hospital, impatient for news of Shannon's condition. After a while, Mac tapped Mitch on the shoulder, shoved a cup of coffee at him and said, "Sit down. You're making me dizzy."

Mitch sat, sipped his coffee. Mac muttered something under his breath. "What did you say?"

"I said that woman is going to send me to an early grave."

"I know what you mean."

Mac studied him for a moment. "You ain't blaming yourself for what happened to her, are you?"

Mitch shrugged.

"Because what happened to her," Mac went on, "is nobody's fault but Shannon's. Don't take that one on. This is who she is, you got nothing to say about it."

"But maybe I could have—"

Mac cut him off. "Look, you wanna carry all that guilt about your family, fine. But if you add Shannon to the list, well then you're either a martyr or a fool. And that's all I have to say about it."

At that moment, the doctor appeared, smiling. Shannon would be fine. The wound had been deep, but had hit nothing of major importance. She'd needed several stitches and one pint of blood, but her recovery would be rapid. She'd be stiff for a while and would spend the night in the hospital but could go home the next day.

Mitch closed his eyes and gave thanks to whatever might be out there. A grinning Carmen gave him a hug. J.R. and Mac nodded at him. There had been an automatic acceptance into this group, strangers to him until two days ago, and it felt strange, yet comforting—a feeling he thought he could get used to, given half a chance.

At home the next day, Shannon was grumpy and feeling just a bit sorry for herself. "I hate this," she told Carmen, who sat on a chair next to her bed. "I hate feeling helpless. I hate being taken care of."

Carmen seemed unfazed. "But your man out there is taking such good care of you, I would think you'd lie back and enjoy it."

"He's not my man."

"Sure he is. And you'll let this one stay."

"Has he said anything to you about that? About me?" Oh, God, she sounded like some high-school kid whispering to her friend at her locker.

"Nope, but he's the one, Shannon."

"Why? I mean, what's different about him?"

"He's strong. He can put up with you, keep up with you. You've never had a man who could do that. Besides, I like him. J.R. does, too. He's the one."

"Don't start getting all smug on me, now that you're married and expecting. You're still my baby sister, and you've never claimed to be able to see into the future."

"I don't have to do that. All I need to do is see the way your face changes when you talk about him, and how his face changes when he looks at you."

The door of the bedroom opened and Mitch came in carrying a tray with soup and muffins on it. "Lupe brought her albondigas soup over and it's delicious."

Carmen rose from her chair. "I'm going to call Mom again, see if I can talk her out of coming down from Santa Barbara tonight. You're in good hands." She beamed a smile at Mitch, then glided out of the room.

"I hate being taken care of," Shannon said.

"Tough." He set the tray down on the bedside table. "Do you want me to feed you?"

"What are you, nuts?"

He shook his head. "Most victims of knife wounds are meek and tired and all too grateful to have someone bring them delicious food. But no, I get to take care of a grump." He sat on the chair just vacated by Carmen. "How are you feeling?"

"I hurt."

"Yeah, I know. Convalescence is not fun. I was in a similar position weeks ago, remember?"

"How could I forget?" She sighed. "Okay, I'll eat."

She reached over and broke off a piece of the muffin top, put it in her mouth, chewed. She looked up. Mitch was looking at her in the oddest way. She swallowed. "What?"

He reached over, tenderness on his face, stroked her cheek. "I almost lost you."

"But you didn't. And it's not your fault, okay?"

"That's what Mac said."

"Well, Mac's right. And furthermore, it's time you faced the fact that your wife and child's death were not your fault either. Joan was mentally ill, Mitch. Then she fell in with unscrupulous people who murdered her to get her money and to keep her quiet. Your son was one of life's casualties, a byproduct of that murder, a terrible, terrible tragedy, but not your fault, do you hear? What good is guilt, I mean, seriously, what does it accomplish? Does it make the world a better place? Can you use the energy created by guilt for good? It's a cop-out."

"Wait just a—"

She held up hand. She'd wanted to say this for a while and now she was going to get it all out. "And you get no credit for my mistakes. I'm the one who wanted to go after JonahDawn. I'm the one who took the chances, who put myself in harm's way, not you. I did it because it was the only way I know how to do things—all out, no holding back. It's the way I fell in love with you."

Again he tried to speak, again she held up her hand to stop him. "No, it's okay. I'm fine if you don't feel quite as deeply as I feel. I mean, my feelings are my responsibility not yours. If I have to, I'll get over them. You're not to blame, you don't have to have any guilt, any burdens, just because I love you."

With that, she expelled a huge breath, then said, "There!"

She reached over and grabbed some more muffin top.

Mitch waited a good long moment before saying quietly, "Are you done yet?"

She cocked her head to one side, thought about it. "You know, I think I am."

"Good, because for once in your life you are going to shut up and listen to someone else."

Her eyes widened with surprise, but he plunged right in, his face grim with resolve. "A. I do bear some blame for what happened to Joan and Jamie, but I also know that most of it was out of my hands. I like to be in control but I had no control over what happened out here to them. I will feel sad and probably somewhat guilty about it for a long time, but I'll survive. B. I wish I could have gotten to Jonah before he hurt you. It was a nightmare, like it was happening all over again to someone I love and I was helpless. I don't like being helpless any better than you do."

"What did you say?"

"Be quiet—"

"Yes sir."

"—because I'm about to get to C. Don't tell me you love me and it's fine if I don't feel the same way, that you'll get over it. You're not supposed to get over being in love. And why do you need to get over it? I'm in love with you, too, you idiot. If you could take some time out of your busy day and your busy life and your busy lawsuits and your busy mouth, you would have seen the signs a while ago. Why am I out here in the land of the fruits and nuts?"

"Why?"

"To be with you."

"Oh."

"Yeah, 'Oh.' Do you think I actually needed to oversee the investigation, your lawsuits? No I did not. I am not a lawyer, thank you God. You are. I am here because you are here."

She stared at him openmouthed and mute, head spinning.

"What's the matter? Cat got your tongue? Lost the power of speech? Finally found something or someone who can shut you up?"

A small grin began to take over her face. "Okay, those are fighting words."

"Bet your ass they are. Now sit back and eat your soup. All of it. I can't hug you because it will hurt you and, as long as you and I live, hopefully for a long, long time and hopefully together, I will never willingly hurt you again. Got that?"

"Yes," she said, in the tiniest voice.

"Good. I'm going out there to visit with your sister."

He left the room then, closing the door behind him.

She sat back, put her spoon in the soup, brought the spoon to her mouth. She supposed if Lupe had made it, it was good. But she didn't really taste it.

What she wanted to do was to call Mitch back in, ask him to go over some of the choice phrases in his little speech, the ones containing words like *I'm in love with you, you idiot,* and that last part, the one where he said something about the two of them living together. *Hopefully together* had been his exact words, and *for a long, long time.*

She grinned. She didn't need to call him back in. She was pretty sure she knew exactly what he'd said.

And why push him any more than she had already, poor man, with all he'd had to put up with. He ought to have the last word.

For now.

*   *   *   *   *

Texas Hold 'Em

When it comes to love, the stakes are high

Sixteen years ago, Luke Chisum dated
Becky Parker on a dare…before going
on to break her heart. Now the former
River Bluff daredevil is back, rekindling
desire and tempting Becky to pick up
where they left off. But this time she has
to resist or Luke could discover the secret
she's kept locked away all these years.…

Look for

TEXAS BLUFF

by Linda Warren

#1470

*Available February 2008
wherever you buy books.*

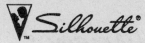

Romantic
SUSPENSE

**Sparked by Danger,
Fueled by Passion.**

When Tech Sergeant Jacob "Mako" Stone opens
his door to a mysterious woman without a past,
he knows his time off is over. As threats to Dee's
life bring her and Jacob together, she must set
aside her pride and accept the help of the military
hero with too many secrets of his own.

Out of Uniform
by Catherine Mann

Available February wherever you buy books.

REQUEST YOUR FREE BOOKS!

2 FREE NOVELS PLUS 2 FREE GIFTS!

Silhouette® Romantic

SUSPENSE

Sparked by Danger, Fueled by Passion!

YES! Please send me 2 FREE Silhouette® Romantic Suspense novels and my 2 FREE gifts. After receiving them, if I don't wish to receive any more books, I can return the shipping statement marked "cancel." If I don't cancel, I will receive 4 brand-new novels every month and be billed just $4.24 per book in the U.S., or $4.99 per book in Canada, plus 25¢ shipping and handling per book plus applicable taxes, if any*. That's a savings of at least 15% off the cover price! I understand that accepting the 2 free books and gifts places me under no obligation to buy anything. I can always return a shipment and cancel at any time. Even if I never buy another book from Silhouette, the two free books and gifts are mine to keep forever.

240 SDN EEX6 340 SDN EEYJ

Name _____ (PLEASE PRINT)

Address _____ Apt. #

City _____ State/Prov. _____ Zip/Postal Code

Signature (if under 18, a parent or guardian must sign)

Mail to the Silhouette Reader Service™:
IN U.S.A.: P.O. Box 1867, Buffalo, NY 14240-1867
IN CANADA: P.O. Box 609, Fort Erie, Ontario L2A 5X3

Not valid to current Silhouette Intimate Moments subscribers.

Want to try two free books from another line?
Call 1-800-873-8635 or visit www.morefreebooks.com.

* Terms and prices subject to change without notice. NY residents add applicable sales tax. Canadian residents will be charged applicable provincial taxes and GST. This offer is limited to one order per household. All orders subject to approval. Credit or debit balances in a customer's account(s) may be offset by any other outstanding balance owed by or to the customer. Please allow 4 to 6 weeks for delivery.

Your Privacy: Silhouette is committed to protecting your privacy. Our Privacy Policy is available online at www.eHarlequin.com or upon request from the Reader Service. From time to time we make our lists of customers available to reputable firms who may have a product or service of interest to you. If you would prefer we not share your name and address, please check here. ☐

SRS07

You can lead a horse to water...

When Alyssa Barkley and Clint Westmoreland
found out that their "fake" marriage was never
rendered void, they are forced to live together
for thirty days. However, Clint loves the single
life and has no intention of being tamed, but
when Alyssa moves in, the sizzling attraction
between them is ignited and neither wants the
thirty days to end.

Look for

TAMING CLINT
WESTMORELAND

by

BRENDA
JACKSON

Available February wherever you buy books

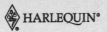

Silhouette® Romantic
SUSPENSE

COMING NEXT MONTH

#1499 CAVANAUGH HEAT—Marie Ferrarella
Cavanaugh Justice

It's been years since Chief of Detectives Brian Cavanaugh has seen his former partner Lila McIntyre, and he's surprised to discover their chemistry is as hot as ever. But he banks down his emotions in order to help Lila catch the stalker who has been harassing her…and discovers a secret that threatens their lives.

#1500 MATCH PLAY—Merline Lovelace
Code Name: Danger

OMEGA undercover agent Dayna Duncan jumps at an undercover assignment overseas. What she doesn't expect is to find former lover USAF pilot Luke Harper awaiting her arrival. A forced reunion may be the only way Dayna and Luke can keep up their aliases, but can they withstand their attraction long enough to complete their mission?

#1501 OUT OF UNIFORM—Catherine Mann
Wingmen Warriors

When Tech Sergeant Jacob "Mako" Stone opens his door to a mysterious woman without a past, he knows his time off is over. As threats to Dee's life bring her and Jacob together, she must set aside her pride and accept the help of the military hero with too many secrets of his own.

#1502 THE PASSION OF SAM BROUSSARD—Maggie Price
Dates with Destiny

A hot lead on a cold case homicide teams up Officer Sam Broussard and OCPD sergeant Liz Scott. Although Sam has never met Liz, there's something very familiar about her. While they uncover the mysteries surrounding the murder, Liz and Sam discover a past neither one remembers sharing...and a killer bent on separating them for eternity.

SRSCNM0108